VAMPIRE
OF THE SKIES

VAMPIRE OF THE SKIES

by

JAMES CORBETT

Introduced by

JOHN PELAN

RAMBLE HOUSE
2014

ISBN 13: 978-1-60543-781-1

Preparation: Gavin L. O'Keefe and Fender Tucker

Dancing Tuatara Press #49

DEDICATED

TO

MY FRIEND CAPTAIN ARTHUR SKEMP

(late Professor of English at Bristol University)

WHO WAS KILLED

A FEW DAYS BEFORE THE ARMISTICE.

"If ye break faith with us
who die
We will not sleep though
poppies grow
In Flanders fields."

JAMES CORBETT

(ex/Lieutenant/3rd & 18th Welsh Regt.

Staff Officer/No. 3 Officers Cadet Battn.)

and Pilot/Royal Flying Corps.)

JAMES CORBETT — A SECOND LOOK

"The man in the grey suit looked uneasy, but his features soon regained control . . ." There aren't too many authors that could (or would) write a line like that with a straight face. The late suspense author James Corbett was one who could (and did) come up with lines like that on a frighteningly regular basis. The author of scores of mysteries from the 1930s through the 1950s, Corbett comes in for a (mostly well-deserved) drubbing by my colleague Bill Pronzini in *Son of Gun in Cheek,* where he describes one of the author's best-known books (*The Merrivale Mystery*) as being "as exciting as watching grass grow." If this is truly the case, then what on earth am I doing including at least two books by the late author in the Dancing Tuatara Press line-up, which has my name (and reputation for whatever that's worth) on it? Was Corbett really that bad? If so, why preserve his work?

The answer is what I call the Lionel Fanthorpe syndrome, (something that may also be extended to the two Arthurs of weird menace fame, Burks and Zagat). There's a tremendous amount of dross, so much so that only a dedicated reader could be expected to wade through it all to find the gems. For those unfamiliar with Mr. Fanthorpe, he was a British author of science fiction, fantasy, and horror who churned out a remarkable volume of (mostly) forgettable work in the 1950s and 1960s. However, buried among hideously bad stories are a substantial volume's worth of weird tales that can stand alongside the best those two decades had to offer. Granted, this is less than 5% of his overall output and so bad is the reputation that it would be exceedingly difficult getting any publisher enthused about producing the book, but the fact remains, there's a good 350 pages or so of Lionel Fanthorpe weird tales that I'd be happy to put up on my shelf with books by acknowledged masters of the form.

This same phenomenon is present in the works of Arthur J. Burks and Arthur Leo Zagat. Both wrote a tremendous amount of material in several genres and when they were off, they were pretty dismal. However, when they were in their element (which for both proved to be the weird menace genre), they were excellent. Reading Burks' science fiction and then turning to a masterpiece such as "The Bells of Oceana" it's hard to imagine that they were written by the same man. Arthur Leo Zagat has been pretty much ignored until recent years, primarily due to his one volume of science fiction *Seven out of Time* that served to sully his reputation for decades. This same phenomenon can be found in the work of James Corbett.

If you consult your Bleiler index, you'll see a handful of novels designated as supernatural in nature, with two others, (*The Hound of Death* and the present volume), both examples of the rationalized supernatural tale popularized by authors such as Walter S. Masterman. Of those, I've found *The Monster of Dagenham Hall* and the present volume to be quite good, with *The Man Who Saw the Devil* and *The Ghost Plane* also well worth reading. The present volume, *Vampire of the Skies,* despite its non-supernatural resolution is filled with plenty of thrills for the fan of the weird menace genre.

One of the things that the author does very well is to sharply delineate his characters, such as the team that assembles to solve the mystery of the young woman drained of blood and thrown from an airplane. We have the stolid local constable, the initial discoverer of the crime, P.C. Gutteridge and the two expert criminologists brought in by Scotland Yard, Malcolm Dacre, and from the French Sûreté, M. Paul Cambon. In fact, it is the dialogue between Dacre and his French colleague that drives the narrative and provides the occasional touch of humor in what is otherwise a fairly grim tale.

So, in the final analysis we have the case of an author who was often mired in mediocrity and who has been often set up as a figure of fun for some of his more outrageous metaphors and similes but who also managed to author over three dozen mysteries, with fully one third of them still quite entertaining today. Is Corbett going to be to the taste of every modern reader? Likely not, throughout his entire career his books are characterized by bizarre plot-twists and what may seem to many readers as an overabundance of dialogue, as characters hammer out the details of the mystery and generally plant several red herrings.

Corbett really seemed to be at his best during the early 1930s and it was during this time period that most of his supernatural or borderline supernatural work was produced. It would appear that market conditions led him to be less adventurous as time went on, a shame really, as when he was on his game, James Corbett could spin a very entertaining (if highly improbable) yarn. We'll be publishing at least a half dozen of his best novels, pretty much evenly divided between straightforward mysteries (from the Ramble House imprint) and weird menace (from Dancing Tuatara Press). I think most readers will agree with me that despite the occasional clunky turn of phrase, there's a lot to enjoy in Corbett's better books and *Vampire of the Skies* makes for an excellent starting point.

John Pelan
Ides of March 2014
Gallup, NM

VAMPIRE OF THE SKIES

CHAPTER I

A SENSATIONAL CRIME

POLICE-CONSTABLE GUTTERIDGE swore a profound oath.

The airplane kept buzzing round him in the sky, just like an enormous kite, except the whir of its wings was more deadly, and the roar of its engine something no kite ever produced.

It was Saturday afternoon, and the district the quiet hamlet of Cottingdale, fifteen miles outside Weymouth. That being so, P.C. Gutteridge had a grievance against that airplane. What was more important, had he encountered the pilot he would have sent him to Hades in no unequivocal language. Saturday afternoon in Cottingdale, during the month of August, between the hours of three and five, usually means a period of quiet. True, there was a game of cricket a mile distant—a friendly match between Ferndale and Cottingdale—at which four hundred spectators were present, but there was nothing else to disturb the calm of Cottingdale. Nothing except that confounded airplane.

Gutteridge stared up at the Thing again.

It had circled round him seventeen times, at a distance of two thousand feet—well, that was as near as he could judge—and the pilot seemed unable to get out of that circular spin. That was the impression he conveyed at least, for the airplane buzzed round Gutteridge till he was almost dizzy, barely slanting its wings when it made the turn, and completing the circle with a faultless swoop. It did not attempt any looping—it was respectable in that sense—but the pilot seemingly imagined he was encircling the earth, with P.C. Gutteridge as the centre of the circumference.

Gutteridge was a burly constable.

His Christian name was Silas, and he weighed sixteen stone without looking round. But that was a secret between himself and the Force. Nowadays policemen are supposed to go in for "slimming," so that if a "speedcop" happens to take neuralgia, or feels dizzy after travelling at 120, an ordinary foot policeman may be requisitioned. P.C. Gutteridge envied every "speed-cop," because speed was the thing he desired, and a policeman cannot sprint at sixteen stone. Not in regulation boots at least.

As the sun shone in all its glory, and as P.C. Gutteridge had tramped Cottingdale roads for two solid hours, he might have been excused for feeling hot. As a matter of truth, he was perspiring. He had used up three handkerchiefs, and wondered how long he could last on the fourth. There was no chance of a siesta in the shade, for a new Inspector was on duty that afternoon, and Gutteridge had an idea that he was about the Cottingdale district. He hated all inspectors like the devil. There was a reasonable chance of compromise with a sergeant, but an inspector demanded the full rigour of the law. P.C. Gutteridge was "fed-up" with rigour. He was also bored with law. But that was another secret between himself and the Force.

This confounded airplane made him sick. First it made him furiously angry, then apoplectic, then diabolically insane with rage, and for the last quarter of an hour it affected his stomach. That circumlocutory motion gave him a pain in his "little Mary"! There was no sense in it. Why the pilot did not move off in another direction was impossible to guess. To keep buzzing round in that eternal circle seemed the clearest evidence of insanity. Gutteridge was used to airplanes. They hovered about at certain intervals, giving him an occasional thrill, but this one took both the bun and the biscuit.

Then something happened.

Had P.C. Gutteridge been an aristocrat and possessed a monocle, he might have inserted it in one eye, for what occurred then was sensational. Nay, it was utterly unprecedented!

The airplane gave a curious dive—not a nose-dive but a stupendous flop—quivered as if it had got out of control, or as if about to shed one of its wings, then a black object hurtled through the air, ejected from the plane itself, and kept on hurtling towards the earth, until finally it dropped on top of a hayrick, in a field not thirty yards from where Gutteridge stood.

Afterwards the airplane soared into the heavens, darted behind an enormous bank of clouds, and was soon lost to sight.

The constable noted that fact, for he stared after the machine like a man in a stupor. He was absolutely dazed by the occurrence, for in all his career as a police-constable he had never witnessed a human body flung from an airplane. Literally flung, for he had distinctly seen the two hands of the pilot, and those two hands had flung out a human body. But it was like throwing out a sack of flour. There had been no struggle of any kind.

P.C. Gutteridge produced his notebook. It was a purely automatic movement, to which he reacted in moments of great stress, but it meant galvanic action of a sort, and it helped to start the thought-process in his brain. He jotted down the time carefully. The hour was 3.30. He put down the date also. It was the second Saturday in August. To aid his memory, he added the words, "Cottingdale *v.* Ferndale," which proved a cricket match was in progress at the time.

Then he returned both watch and notebook to their respective pockets, paused for a few more seconds in complete bewilderment, then marched towards the hayrick with an air of dramatic intensity. It meant traversing the open road for a few more yards, and whilst engaged in that task, he noticed there was no other human being within sight. Apparently he was the only individual who had witnessed the awful tragedy. The thing took his breath away. What a report he would have for the new Inspector!

When he entered the field containing the hayrick, he saw that Fortune had favoured him to a certain extent. It was one of those square, modern hayricks, built to measurement and design, and almost the size of a house. But, as if anticipating the perplexity of P.C. Gutteridge, a long ladder lay at the side of it, and the constable breathed a prayer of gratitude. Would the ladder bear his sixteen stone? He decided to put it to the test. This was where enormous strength came to his aid. He had no difficulty raising the ladder, or in placing it against the hayrick, but, when it came to mounting it, he wiped the perspiration from his brow.

What would he find up there?

Then he thought of England and Horatio Nelson, of Drake, Cabot, and Mussolini, of the multifarious regulations of the British Police Force, of the Westminster Confession of Faith, and sundry little oddments, then perspired up the ladder.

This was a great day in his life.

It seemed an eternity before he reached the top, for he was in no hurry to get there, but at last he was within sight of the final rung, then he stopped like one stricken with heart disease. For his eyes beheld something that gave him a sickening gasp of horror, and so great was his astonishment that he almost collapsed.

A woman's body lay before him—a remarkably young woman—and the upper part of her shoulder was quite bare. The eyes were closed in death. But the breast revealed a gaping knife-wound, and all her clothes were bespattered with blood. Never had Gutteridge beheld a more horrible sight, for that knife-wound was of prodigious size, and all round it were the marks of animal-like teeth. The murderer had actually drank his victim's blood. There could be no other explanation of those ghoulish teeth-marks, and even Gutteridge saw that in a brilliant flash. Had it been possible, he would have produced his notebook afresh, but the scene was too horrible for human eyes, and slowly he descended the ladder.

He knew he should have gone back, mounted the hayrick, and made a more minute examination. But a crime of this magnitude did not occur every day and, to be frank, poor Gutteridge had lost his nerve.

He was totally bewildered by his discovery. The whole business seemed like a ghastly nightmare of the brain, in which a mad pilot and a fiendish airplane figured throughout, and had a bottle of brandy been handy, he would have drained it at one gulp. Then he did a most extraordinary thing. Without pause, without waiting another second, he produced the whistle from his tunic and blew it with all the energy his lungs possessed. And he went on blowing it, caring little for the fool he looked, or for the pandemonium of chaos he created, and probably he would have gone on blowing that whistle for another fifteen minutes had something not appeared before his vision. He stopped suddenly. It was the new Inspector.

"What the blazes has happened?" the latter asked. "Do you imagine that hayrick is on fire, or have you taken sunstroke? What is it, Gutteridge? You have been blowing that whistle for nearly five minutes! What the devil is wrong? Answer me! Don't stand there like a stuffed owl. What is it? Can't you speak? Have you gone completely daft?" Inspector Frank Murray was highly indignant. He had heard the whistle when nearly a mile away, and had run at breakneck speed to the scene. Other people were running also—farmers, labourers, tourists, a whole crowd of cricket spectators! Why, all Cottingdale would be there in a minute!

P.C. Gutteridge found breath at last.

He came to a sharp salute.

But he lost none of his dignity. His face remained quite solemn. With a trembling hand, he pointed to the top of the hayrick.

"It's murder!" he said in an awful voice. "Young lady thrown from an airplane, sir. Saw it myself with my own eyes. Stabbed in the breast—and the brute has drunk her blood! Yes, ghastly, it makes me sick! Go up and have a look for yourself!"

A little crowd had collected. They were just in time to hear the last words from the police-constable. They stared at him in amazement. Inspector Murray was plainly embarrassed. In all his official experience, he had never dealt with a mad constable. It was palpable P.C. Gutteridge was a raving lunatic. However, it was best to humour him. He would have to be led gently away, and if he would not come quietly—!

"Go up and see for yourself!" Gutteridge repeated in the same awestruck voice. "You may think I'm balmy—I thought so myself when I saw the body pushed from the plane—but go up that ladder and have a peep. Then you will realise what has happened. It's a case for the Yard, Inspector, and the sooner we get in touch with Headquarters the better!"

Murray pulled himself together. The word "Yard" convinced him that Gutteridge was not play-acting. As the crowd increased and pushed forward, all talking at once, he made up his mind and took a dive at the ladder. He mounted it in a remarkably short space of time. Then he held up his hand for silence. The crowd below became as quiet as tame mice. No one ventured to breathe. Inspector Murray took another solemn glance at that murdered form on top of the hayrick, then turned to those beneath.

"Ask someone to run for a doctor!" he said breathlessly. "The constable is quite right. A young woman is lying here murdered—brutally stabbed to death—but I think a doctor should be found. We will want his evidence in any case. Gutteridge, come up here and let us have a look round. You are perfectly in order when you said it was a case for the Yard! I will phone through at once!"

He had climbed on top of the hayrick, and Gutteridge was soon beside him. In the presence of his official superior, he could manifest fine courage. He looked down at the crowd beneath, held up his hand as if stopping all traffic, and uttered a warning in a loud, stentorian voice.

"Keep quiet down there!" he bawled. "Don't you understand plain English? This is a case for Scotland Yard, and nothing is going to be touched. Keep them back a distance of ten yards, Farmer Jackson, and if anyone ventures up that ladder, it is going to cost him a fine of five pounds. No one must come up here except Dr. Philip Gibbs. Farmer Wilson, send your boy for him at once, and don't stand gaping up at me like a cow! Yes, Johnnie Maxwell, I said Dr. Gibbs, and run like hell's fire!"

Johnnie Maxwell ran like hell's fire!

Farmer Wilson hitched up his corduroy breeches. Away back in his subconscious brain was a vague recollection of the duties of a Special Constable. To do it properly, of course, it required an armlet. Nevertheless, England expected every man—Assuming an attitude of tremendous importance, he advanced to the crowd and pushed it back. He even asked the cricket people, in none too polite language, to stop using their voices like a human gramophone, and suggested if they kept their mouths shut they would not catch cold!

Meanwhile Inspector Murray was busy. He was the modern, athletic type, firm-chested, and full of vitality. His own notebook was out, and he was writing vigorously. He saw the victim was a plain-looking girl about twenty-five, that she wore a light brown mackintosh and no hat. Her dark hair was shingled, and some of it streamed about in disorder. And, as Gutteridge had already noted, her blouse and clothes were covered with blood. He examined the gaping knife-wound, saw the marks of the animal-like teeth, and, at the sight, even Murray shuddered.

"Heavens above," he exclaimed in a tone of horror, "do you see that, Gutteridge? Why, the brute has buried his teeth in her flesh! God, what was the ghastly idea? Do you want me to believe he actually drank her blood? Ugh, it's preposterous! And yet—and yet—! Good Lord, I believe you are right. I honestly think that is what happened. He stabbed her first—a terrific stab with some murderous knife—then, like some human vampire, he drank her life-blood!"

Gutteridge looked up aloft.

"A vampire!" he muttered. "Yes, a vampire of the skies! I wish he'd only come back. I wish he'd land in this field.

But the skunk flew away behind that bank of clouds. I watched him out of sight. But I could hardly believe my eyes. I tell you I saw him fling the body out of the plane. I saw his two naked hands. I saw him lean over the cockpit—"

Inspector Murray stared at him aghast. The full significance of the Thing was just beginning to dawn on him. An airplane! Gutteridge actually saw this thing happen! Saw the murderer shoot the girl out of his machine! Why, Gutteridge would be chief witness for the Crown! His photograph would be in all the papers. He would be a national hero!

"Say, Gutteridge," he half-shouted, "you're not pulling my leg, are you? You haven't invented a cock-and-bull story for the sake of the Yellow Press, have you? Sure you haven't been struck with a heat wave? The sun was exceptionally strong at one o'clock, and you are no youngster. Your avoirdupois is growing no less, old man, and it's the easiest thing in the world to get a brain-stroke! Why, out in the Channel Islands last year—"

P.C. Gutteridge looked at his superior with sublime pity.

It was a withering look, and Inspector Murray quailed.

"It's not my job to inspect hayricks, sir!" he said proudly. "I don't go round climbing ladders and looking for dead bodies at my time of life. I'm a respectable police-constable, Inspector, with almost twenty years' service to my credit, and I have never been accused of sunstroke! That is a reflection on personal character, sir, and, at the very least, I think I am entitled to an apology!"

Inspector Murray apologised. He did so with a very bad grace, but he recalled that Gutteridge was a Crown witness, and, as such, must be placated at all cost.

"On the other hand," he countered, "British pilots don't make a practice of chucking girls out of airplanes. You must admit, Gutteridge, I am straining my imagination to believe you. If that poor girl had to be murdered, it would have been a far easier job to do it on Mother Earth. Why take her up four thousand feet to stick a knife in her? . . . But if you are prepared to swear—"

"I am prepared to kiss the Holy Bible, sir!" was the solemn answer. "I tell you I saw the brute lean over the machine, then push that girl right out into space! The whole thing occurred in a flash, but I had my eye on him, Inspector—I had my eye on him!"

Murray whistled. Then he got to work again. He made a more rigorous survey of the girl's clothes, found no papers or letters to establish her identity, and again made entries in his notebook. P.C. Gutteridge copied his example with all promptitude, keeping a careful eye on the crowd below to see the ten-yard limit had not been exceeded, and feeling in the mood for three strong glasses of brandy. That gaping knife-wound—with all that it suggested—sent him cold and shivery, and he began to wish that Dr. Gibbs would arrive.

That individual came along in seven minutes.

The crowd parted for him like one man.

"What the devil's all the fuss about?" he blazed irritably. He had just been awakened from an afternoon nap, in which the State had trebled the amount of panel insurance, and the shock of reality was terrible. He was not in the best of tempers. Besides, like Gutteridge, he was of slightly Herculean proportion, and all this rush sent the blood to his head. When he mounted the ladder he resembled an enraged walrus!

Inspector Murray pointed to the dead body.

"A case for the Yard!" he said briefly. "I want your official report, doctor. This is Police-Constable Gutteridge, one of the smartest members of Cottingdale Police Station—not that I should say it. But he has demonstrated his genius this afternoon. He has just told me a most remarkable story, but I am quite prepared to believe it. That young woman has been murdered, doctor, and the constable saw her body flung from an airplane. Yes, saw it with his own eyes . . . A very shrewd piece of work on his part!"

It is doubtful if the doctor was listening.

He was far too practical a man for fairy stories, and his whole gaze was concentrated on the murdered body.

Then, his professional instinct at work, he dropped on his knees in the hay, and examined the fatal knife-wound with a penetrating stare. He marvelled at the size of the wound, at the cruel depth of it, at the jagged twist which the knife made in being withdrawn, then he started to his feet with a gasp of horror. The animal-like teeth caught his attention. He saw the meaning of it. He saw what had happened, what the murderer had done.

"Father of saints," he exclaimed, "do you see what the brute has done! Whoever murdered this poor girl is a ghoul or vampire in human form! After stabbing her with some murderous knife, he has sucked the blood right from the wound, just like some fiendish animal of the jungle! My God, I can hardly stand the sight!"

Once more he bent down, not listening to the comments of the Inspector, but concentrating all his wits on the murdered girl. He noted the bloodstained clothes, the disordered hair, the bespattered blouse. Then he rose to his feet and scratched his head.

"What the devil is the meaning of it?" he gasped. "Who has done this?"

He looked down at the crowd as if trying to pick out the murderer, and Inspector Murray flashed him a look of sorrow.

"I have been trying to tell you, doctor!" he said impressively. "This is P.C. Gutteridge—"

The Cottingdale medico swore impatiently.

"Dear God, I've known Gutteridge twenty years!" he shouted. "But I don't know you, sir. You are a stranger to this neighbourhood. You are one of our new County Inspectors, eh? Well, you want an introduction, not my friend Gutteridge. Now, Silas, spin out the story. No fables, mind. How in the name of Madagascar did you come across this body, and what the devil made you suspect it was on top of a hayrick!"

P.C. Gutteridge expanded the full size of his massive chest. At that instant he looked Herculean. Someone below raised a faint cheer. Against the sky, the three figures on the hayrick looked dramatic, almost absurd, but the comic side did not appeal to them. All three men were horribly in earnest. Underneath the crowd gaped up, each man whispering to his neighbour the latest version of the murder. In vain did Farmer Jackson press them back; they seethed forward like a human battering-ram. Cottingdale would not forget this scene for three generations.

"Gibbs," said Gutteridge ponderously, "I have known you twenty years. You have never found me out in a lie, have you, sir?"

"Never, Gutteridge!" The reply was prompt and galvanic.

Gutteridge expanded another inch. He could just do it.

"Then believe it or not," he said, "but I saw that poor wench flung out of an airplane at half-past three this afternoon. I've got the time down in my notebook. Have a look for yourself!"

Dr. Gibbs gave the Inspector a ponderous wink.

"Good Mother Hubbard," he groaned, "another tragedy! Poor old Gutteridge. Poor old Gutteridge! Gone clean potty, and due for his pension in six months!"

CHAPTER II

THE DEVIL'S HANDIWORK

WELL, the Yard sent down Malcolm Dacre.

That act, in itself, showed intelligence. Manifestly, Scotland Yard proved itself a going concern. But it has been going a long time.

It certainly meant the crime was super-important, for Dacre was the most brilliant man at Headquarters. He shone at every angle. It was the Birmingham case that made him famous, where Reuben Morrison, a well-known jeweller, was found with his throat cut. Dacre disposed of the suicide theory. He brought the crime home to the man's sister. It was a case of clever deduction and analysis, for the motive was difficult to prove, but the Yard man furnished evidence of guilt, and after climbing that pinnacle of distinction, he never looked back.

There was no swank with Dacre.

He was not the clever-clever type who conceal their brains, who wear them under a mask. That kind is found in fiction. Nowadays, from the boots upward, the Yard Big Five demand intelligence. They are tired of "chumps." It must be intelligence of a superlative degree, with not the faintest doubt about the grey matter.

Malcolm Dacre was what he looked.

He never tried to look otherwise. He was an intellectual, and, with it all, he was genuinely modest. There was real discernment in his dark, glowing eyes, and the trick he had of bringing his lips together boded ill for any chance suspect. He had passed his thirtieth birthday, and, for some reason known only to the gods, had remained unmarried. He was a cynic with a peculiar philosophy. In his judgment, the marital state did not suit his profession. That is, he never knew the moment he would be shot, or murdered according to modern Inquisition rules, so, if he had to die suddenly, he preferred dying as a respectable bachelor.

Dacre was eminently respectable. He had a strict code, and he never flinched from it. He had little sentiment, for Life had taught him a stern lesson, and, strange to state, his biggest disillusionment came from the opposite sex. Girls were anathema to him. In some funny way, arranged possibly by a malevolent Fate, the majority of people he arrested, for one crime or another, did not wear trousers. They wore skirts, and short ones at that. Which convinced him, if he needed conviction, that Eve must have been an arch-priestess of Evil.

Yet Malcolm Dacre had a handsome face and figure. His splendid shoulders marked him down as an athlete, and he knew how to dress. The women admitted that grudgingly. They hated him—apparently—because he hated them! Yet despite his cynicism, his personality was attractive to women. Indeed his notoriety as a woman-hater only made matters worse. When disengaged from the stress of Yard work—and even murderers have a breathing space—Dacre was invited to many Society functions, at which he yawned politely, being always too modest to keep away. He went to those functions, he told his Chief, to study Society "in the deepest pink," to get a glimpse behind the curtain, and, of course, the experience made him a greater cynic than ever.

Still he had lifted Yard prestige. Sir Francis Didgett, the Chief, thought him unique, and so he was. Dacre worked hard, and his undimmed intellect made him the terror of evildoers. He had seventeen crime solutions to his credit—"scalps" he called them—and, in every instance, they were murder cases where no clue presented itself. Had he wished, he could have claimed highest promotion. But he was not out for that. He was entitled to Superintendent rank, but he never used it. This proved he was without snobbery. He desired no handle to his name, and told his Chief, jestingly, his coffin would only require initials!

He had a private flat at 3a Curzon Street. That was his only luxury, and because he was unique, he had this privilege.

When the news came through about the Cottingdale murder, Dacre was getting ready for dinner. Not in his flat, bless you, but at the Regal, in Lombard Street. It was to be a modest affair with a Yard colleague, ladies exempt, then possibly a theatre, or, horror of horrors, a visit to the latest Hollywood film. He happened to be free at the moment—the Yard knew that (curses!)—and his holidays were due in a fortnight. Then the Yard Chief sent that peremptory message, and Dacre replied over the phone.

It was a most bewildering phone call—all about a girl being thrown out of an airplane—and Dacre had to restrain a smile. Then the word murder reached his ears, and the smile vanished. His lips closed. The Chief's voice sounded hoarse, and like a thousand miles distant, but he got the details at last, and in twenty minutes was in the Weymouth express. It meant the devil of a race, but he caught it, and, with a subdued chuckle, flung himself in a first-class compartment. Once again he was in harness, and that meant everything. Before midnight, perhaps, he might eat comfortably in a Weymouth hotel, or, peradventure, there might be decent food at Cottingdale. He believed Cottingdale was on the map. He had never heard of it.

Then he went to sleep, and, in some terrible nightmare, dreamt Sir Francis Didgett had metamorphosed into a police-constable. He woke with a wild laugh, and then laughed afresh when he thought of Didgett in a blue uniform. When he reached Weymouth the murder was in all the local papers. He bought one with a grim smile, and knew London editions contained similar news. There was a nauseating photograph of P.C. Gutteridge on the front page, and it frightened him. Yes, all England would be discussing this crime, and the reporters would be round him like flies. That was the curse of it. How he hated publicity. Yet he knew it helped to a tremendous extent.

As regards the crime, he had not thought about it. All the way down in the train, when not sleeping, he had kept his mind averted, for he did not believe in official gossip, or what the "Crime-Editor" thought before his cocktail. Often a murder, when he got in contact, presented quite a different aspect. All the same, P.C. Gutteridge excepted, he had a subconscious sense he was in for a big thrill. A girl flung from an airplane! Well, that did not occur every Saturday. No, by George, it didn't! This would prove the most sensational case of the year.

Then came an interruption.

He had just reached the telegraph office, confirmed that no wires awaited him, when a laughing voice sounded in his ear.

He turned instantly. It was a real surprise. It was no other than M. Paul Cambon, the distinguished member of the French *Sûreté*, who, he remembered, was enjoying a holiday at the moment. Although French to the finger-tips, Cambon dressed and talked like the typical Englishman, and his knowledge of the language was perfect.

He was a tall, broad-shouldered individual, with luminous blue eyes, an enigmatic face, and a wonderful set of teeth. These teeth he showed when he smiled, just like a negro, but when that occurred he was the embodiment of charm. Like Dacre, he was also a bachelor, but he was close on fifty, and his *Sûreté* career was almost over. Dacre he had known for some years, not intimately, but they held each other in respect, and everyone knew Cambon had a fine record.

"Well, that's devilish odd!" he exclaimed after the preliminary greeting. "You see, Dacre, there must be something in telepathy, for I read all about the Cottingdale mystery, and then I got an idea you would be sent. 'Pon my soul, no sooner did the idea enter my head than you emerged from that telegraph office."

"The Fates are kind." Dacre laughed.

"That depends. I have been waiting one hour on a friend from Southampton—may his soul writhe in torment—and he has disappointed me. Well, Dacre, it's splendid to see you again. Look here, I'm staying at Claridge's Hotel, in Weymouth—yes, they have a bathroom—so, for heaven's sake, don't forget to look me up. Not in the bath, of course, but say at supper to-night. Possibly I might offer a suggestion—just one or two—and they might give you an idea. What do you say?"

Dacre was delighted to meet his French colleague. Cambon was a difficult personage—most difficult—but he could be entertaining when he liked, and Dacre had found him agreeable. It was two years since they met. There was much to discuss.

"My dear Cambon," he answered, "I certainly will call. I may even put up there myself—and inspect that bath! I have a car waiting to take me to Cottingdale, but there may be no decent accommodation there, and, like yourself, I always prefer a detached view of things."

M. Cambon presented his cigarette case.

"And the murder?" he queried. "What do you think of it?"

"I have not thought about it. The Chief rang me up at my flat, gave me a few details, and told me I was the man for the job, so here I am. I have just bought a copy of the Weymouth paper, and was going to glance at the latest news when you gave me the surprise of my life!"

M. Cambon laughed.

"I have read the case," he said with a yawn, "but, between ourselves, Dacre, that chap Gutteridge is insane. When you get down there, you will find that is the general belief. I have been speaking to one or two people who have come up from Cottingdale, and that is the prevailing impression. Your poor English constable suffers from sunstroke. Failing that, he must be reading the latest crime stories, and his imagination has got the better of him. Throwing a girl out of an airplane—Well, it does make you sit down and weep, doesn't it?"

Dacre accepted a cigarette with a murmur of thanks. He lit it carefully before he answered.

"Ah, but you forget," he said, "that Gutteridge found the body on top of a hayrick. Now, even assuming the airplane story to be funny, a hayrick is a peculiar place for a murdered body. Is it not so, M. Cambon?"

The Frenchman gave that impressive shrug.

"The murderer may have a passion for hayricks," he smiled. "Personally, I think it was not a bad idea. Hayricks do not walk about. They are stationary objects, and they do not like company. They remain aloof by themselves, unvisited for weeks."

Dacre smiled afresh.

"True," he intervened, "but a country policeman does not go about examining hayricks. Net unless his attention is called to one, and Gutteridge landed on this mystery himself. It is a singular story, friend, but it may contain a substratum of truth. At any rate, I will get the doctor's report, and have a chat with the Chief Constable. If there is any time before midnight, I may get in to Weymouth for supper. That will depend entirely on the fascination of that hayrick!"

The French expert came to a sudden decision.

" 'Pon my soul, I have an idea!" he declared. "Do you mind, Dacre, if I go down with you to Cottingdale? I also have a passion for hayricks, and this case seems interesting. If I can be of service, or if I can prove the insanity of P.C. Gutteridge, then it will be repaying old debts. You have helped us often. It's an offer. Do you accept?"

"With pleasure!" Dacre replied. "It will be fine to have your views, M. Cambon—however we disagree—and, after all, what is more enjoyable than an argument! That car is outside the station. If it's not, someone's going to get a thick ear. And I presume Chief Constable Muir will meet us at Cottingdale. Come along and tell me all about Paris!"

M. Cambon paused.

"*Tiens*," he gasped, "what about dinner? My dear fellow, you have ample time to come back to Claridge's. I have managed the leg of a chicken, two pears, and a drink of Moselle, but I am never hungry. You must be ravenous. Look, I will smoke these Turkish cigarettes while you dine.

What do you say, Dacre? Cottingdale, they tell me, is the last place made by the Creator. They sell nothing but lemonade and ice-cream. You will be starved there for a certainty."

The Yard expert shuddered. Then he laughed again.

"I am an idealist," he replied. "Duty first every time, Monsieur Cambon. I don't mind confessing I am ravenous—almost cannibalistic—but a dinner at Claridge's would mean a delay of twenty minutes, and I must reach Cottingdale before the light fails. If you don't mind, we will go there at once. Here is a car, and the chauffeur looks perfectly sober. Step in, friend, and pray for no accidents."

The chauffeur recognised Dacre instantly. His salute was the correct Army one, and in two seconds the detectives were being whirled along the Weymouth road. Cottingdale was reached in forty minutes, and, as anticipated, the Chief Constable met them outside the station. The car passed that way *en route* for the field in which the murdered body was found, and the chauffeur had received his Instructions.

Dacre introduced M. Cambon. The Chief Constable was profuse in his delight.

"Cottingdale is honoured, my dear sir. If you two gents are tackling the job, Mr. Dacre, then we may expect a solution before midnight." It was a direct compliment, and the experts smiled.

"Not on your life!" M. Cambon protested, "No, Muir, I am merely staying in Weymouth on holiday, and I met Dacre at the railway station. It was my suggestion to come here on a friendly visit. We don't make hayricks in the same fashion—not in France at least—and this Cottingdale hayrick appeals to me. There is something daringly original about this method of murder, Chief Constable, and I may pick up a few hints for the *Sûreté*. So far, airplane crimes have been outside my category, but one never knows, does one!" He laughed loudly, and Dacre was compelled to join in the merriment.

"What is the latest news?" Dacre asked casually. "I read that the body has been removed from the hayrick, and I want to meet this famous constable who masquerades under the name of Gutteridge."

The Chief Constable nodded.

"Everything is ready," he said promptly. "The body has been moved to Farmer Jackson's home—the hayrick belongs to him, and he has supplied a sitting-room—and P.C. Gutteridge, who came off duty at six, is having a bite of food there at present. We had a phone message you were coming, Mr. Dacre, and Gutteridge has been in a flutter ever since. He's feeling quite proud to-night, sir. It's the first time his photo has been in the local papers, and better still, he is a Crown witness"

"Where is Jackson's farm?" Dacre asked.

The Chief Constable jumped in behind.

"Another mile along the road," he answered. "If you don't mind giving me a lift, I will guide you there in a jiffy. Three minutes will do it. Well, Monsieur Cambon, how do you enjoy Weymouth? A little bird tells me you are staying in Claridge's Hotel, but I never dreamt you would be paying us a visit. My word, it's good to have your collaboration."

M. Cambon gave a significant yawn.

"Oh, Weymouth's all right," he replied. "The same delightful seaside resort, and the same conventional young ladies. A lot different to Bournemouth, you know. I may go there next week. It all depends on my mood. I'm a bird of passage this weather. As regards collaboration, Dacre may not want my help after to-night. He will put me down as a confounded nuisance, thank me in the nicest possible terms, and get rid of me as quickly as possible. I would do the same thing. But we will see—we will see. Been long in these parts, Muir?"

"A matter of ten years. I had a transfer from Devon, and I find this county suits me better. But you are quite right about the women folk, M. Cambon. Weymouth must be tame after Juan-les-Pins, eh?"

The Frenchman looked at him hard.

"I believe you're sane," he said in a metallic voice. "Tell me, Muir, you don't believe this story about an airplane?"

The Chief Constable seemed nonplussed. He wanted to be conciliatory and level-headed—to be called sane by M. Cambon was a compliment—but the blue eyes of the Frenchman made him wince.

"Well, sir, I don't know what to think," he confessed. "No crime like this has come within my personal experience. No doubt you have seen the papers. That part about the human vampire is true enough. There is a terrible knife-gash in the young woman's shoulder, just an inch above the breast, and the wound is perfectly horrible. It looks as if someone had been gnawing at it. Actually gnawing at the bare flesh. You can see the marks of human teeth. The murderer was not satisfied with his bestial crime. He deliberately drank the life-blood of his victim!"

M. Cambon seemed tickled to death.

"But let us be serious for one moment," he pleaded. "Muir, I ask you a plain question. This is 1931, and the days of Jules Verne are over. What I want to know is this: do you, as a sensible Chief Constable of the County, believe this ghoulish story about a young woman being thrown out of an airplane? I tell you I don't believe it. To me, the whole thing is nothing but a monstrous fabrication of the mind. And I'm quite prepared to tell Gutteridge that when I see him. No man—not even a lunatic—would commit a crime of that kind. And when you talk of lunatics, *mon ami*, they are a trifle more intelligent than you think."

Dacre flashed him a critical glance.

"Look here, Cambon," he queried, "why the devil are you so dogmatic on that point? The airplane has now become common property. It is used by all kinds of people. Getting a flying licence is comparatively simple—when you know how to fly, and when you can pass the test. Private airplane clubs are scattered all over the show. Your modern pilot is everywhere. He can breakfast at Croydon, lunch in Paris, and dine in Berlin. Incidentally he can commit a murder in that same machine."

M. Cambon threw out his hands in disgust.

"Bah!" he snorted, "not even a lunatic would dispose of the body in that fashion. Look at the trail of evidence he leaves behind! The young woman is bound to be discovered, her identity traced, every fact about her known, how she met the pilot, what induced her to enter the airplane, what aerodrome she visited, what pilots she knew—*Mon Dieu*, the connecting links are too numerous. Believe me, Dacre, our modern murderer is much too clever. His first thought is to clear himself of all suspicion, dispose of the body in the most cunning way, and leave no clue or pointer behind!"

The Chief Constable leaned forward. He stressed the same point as Dacre.

"Yes, but how do you account for Gutteridge finding the body on top of the hayrick?" he asked triumphantly. "Gutteridge is not a detective, M. Cambon. He is just a plain constable, weighs sixteen stone, has little imagination, but has a solid, practical mind. If he says he saw a man throw the body from an airplane, it does sound incredible, but Gutteridge is not a visionary. And certainly it's not his job to go sniffing round hayricks."

M. Cambon sighed.

The stupidity of the English!

"You forget what I said," he replied. "I speak from experience, and Dacre will confirm. Your present-day murderer is astute. His first thought is to dispose of the body, and in the most cunning way possible. My idea is this: that murder was committed in broad daylight, possibly at the lunch hour or immediately after, at least when there were few people about. The field is private, and trespassers are watched in the dark. But in the sunshine it is different. The hayrick was a brilliant idea. The murderer knew the body might not be found for weeks, and, as the ladder was left alongside—that ladder is mentioned in the paper—what was easier than for him to use it? He carried the body on top of the hayrick. Better still, for all you or I know, the murder may have been committed on top of the hayrick. Possibly they were lovers, then a quarrel, and finally the murder. Nothing more plausible. But an airplane . . . Pardon me, Muir, but your Gutteridge is a fool—a damned fool!"

Dacre listened to all this harangue. The words impressed him, but only from a distorted angle. He was pleased the French expert had come to help, to offer criticism, to make a suggestion. But his method of reasoning was illogical. Dacre saw the flaws at once, yet remained silent. It would not do to offend Cambon. After a pause, he observed,

"Well, I believe in Gutteridge," he said doggedly. "Part of my Anglo-Saxon obstinacy, Cambon, but you may be perfectly right. Gutteridge, for all I know, is a damned fool!"

The Frenchman joined in the laugh.

Then the Chief Constable held up his hand.

"Here we are, John," he called out pleasantly. "Do you mean to tell me you don't know Farmer Jackson's hayfield? Gosh, I'm surprised at you . . . Gentlemen, there you are on my right. That is the world-famous hayrick, Mr. Dacre, and, as you see, the ladder still lies against it. That ladder will also go down to history, for on it P.C. Gutteridge climbed to fame . . . Say, look at this crowd already!"

Yes, the crowd of sightseers was tremendous. But most of them clustered round the farm, which contained the body, and which lay another fifty yards down the road. Some six constables cleared a way for the car, saluted the Chief Constable, and made themselves suddenly busy. Few of them recognised the experts, but they had a good suspicion that one was a Yard man.

Dacre turned to the Chief Constable.

"Ask the chauffeur to keep waiting," he begged. "Cambon or I may wish to rush back to Weymouth. I may put up in one of the Cottingdale inns, or take a race down to Claridge's Hotel, Weymouth. That will depend on developments, and what points come to hand."

"Very good, sir!" Muir knew the man he was addressing, and the distinction he held at the Yard.

"And, Chief, get hold of that Dr. Gibbs," Dacre finished. "When you do, send him along to the farm. I want to see his official report, and hear what comments he has to make . . . Now then, Cambon, are you ready for the next venture? Here goes!"

He jumped smartly out, followed by the French expert, and entered the modest farm dwelling. Another constable met them at the door, but he had a warning shout from the Chief, and he sprang to attention.

"Just see we are left undisturbed," Dacre said to him. "And, constable, immediately Dr. Gibbs arrives, send him right in to me!"

"The moment he arrives, sir!"

Farmer Jackson ambled out to them from the passage. His shoulders were getting bent with age, but there was a kindly flash in his brown eyes. He seemed to recognise the visitors, for the constable whispered something to him, and to Dacre he gave a nod of welcome.

"Down from the Yard, sir?" he exclaimed. "Well, I thought as much. Been expecting you this last hour. Thank God that kettle is boiling, so you can have a drop of tea if you feel like it. Or perhaps you want to see that poor creature first? Very well, you will find the body in the sitting-room. And if you can't discover the brute who done that ghoulish murder, then the Creator will find him in His own good time!"

"Never mind the Creator!" M. Cambon said irritably. "Push on, Dacre, and examine the devil's handiwork!"

CHAPTER III

WHAT DID DACRE FIND?

THEN, inside the room, a solitary figure rose to his feet. It was P.C. Gutteridge.

He had heard the commotion outside the window, saw Dacre, whom he recognised from a photograph, and overheard Chief Constable Muir. In a flash he slipped inside the sitting-room. To Farmer Jackson he gave a ponderous wink, showing he realised the importance of the occasion, then took up the position of chief mourner, or rather, sentry on guard.

Was he not the leading Crown witness? Was his portrait not in all the papers? Why, he would be in the *Daily Sketch* on Monday, and *The News of the World* to-morrow! And had he not discovered the body? Was it not due to his marvellous observation, whilst on duty, that the murderer had been detected flinging the victim from an airplane? Why, in all history the affair had no precedent. This meant two more stripes. And if he did not get promotion, he could write to the Home Secretary.

"Good evening, Mr. Dacre!" he said condescendingly. "I'm Gutteridge!"

"Well, I'm damned!" shouted a voice behind Dacre. It belonged to M. Cambon, and obviously he had no idea of P.C. Gutteridge's importance. "So you are the idiot who started the yarn about the airplane? Well, I have come here specially to make your acquaintance. Gutteridge, if you were in my country—I have the honour to refer to France—you would be decorated with the Legion of Honour. They might even confer the *Croix de Guerre*. At any rate, you would have the Blue Riband, and be buried near the Invalides. Yes, Monsieur Gutteridge, you would be a national hero. Your postcard would sell over Europe, you would be filmed in two Continents. But alas in England they do not realise your intellectual stature!"

Dacre took little notice. He had moved across to the sofa, which contained the victim of the sensational crime, then concentrated all his mind on that still figure.

But P.C. Gutteridge had received a shock.

In the first place, he had never met M. Cambon in his life. He did not know what status he possessed, or to whom he sent his laundry, or what connexion he had with the Police Force, or what he was doing in England if he belonged to France. He did not know those things. All he realised was that he had been insulted, and the circumstance demanded an apology. M. Cambon must retract. He would show this insolent Frenchman that P.C. Gutteridge, X437I, of Cottingdale Constabulary, leading witness for the Crown, could not be treated in this manner.

"What the devil do you mean?" he blazed in righteous anger. "If you say another word, I will put you under immediate arrest. You may be a friend of Mr. Dacre, but you are no friend of mine. I belong to the Cottingdale Constabulary, and I know my duty to England. I have the use of mine eyes, my fine fellow, and I have provided fifteen newspaper reporters with copy. Yes, fifteen of them, one after the other, and they all say I acted with outstanding ability. Idiot indeed! I want your apology, sir, and I want it quick!"

M. Cambon fidgeted with his watch-chain. He realised that Dacre was being interrupted in his task, that he was frowning heavily, so he pulled Gutteridge into the deserted kitchen. There he continued the harangue.

"Look here, you blasted fool," he said in a truculent voice—a voice he often used at the *Sûreté*, "if you keep to that story of the airplane, and the mad pilot who chucked the girl out of the cockpit, you are going to become the laughing-stock of England. Do you realise what that means?"

P.C. Gutteridge pushed his massive stomach to the front. He made a frantic endeavour to look dignified. His face went purple with choleric rage. His hands trembled in a righteous passion. He felt there was going to be a second murder. He was certain about it. He wanted to choke this Frenchman, to press his windpipe hard. Never had he heard such insolence, such unpardonable cheek. Who the blazes was the fellow? And why had he come along with Mr. Dacre?

"Say, who the hell are you?" he roared. "Or who do you think you are? Perhaps that's more important."

"It is!" the French expert confided. "And if you want an answer to that question, Gutteridge, I am Paul Cambon, of the French *Sûreté*, and Dacre there will confirm it. Now you realise what a blithering idiot you are!" Yes, M. Cambon had a perfect grasp of the English language. There was not the faintest doubt about it.

P.C. Gutteridge swallowed hard. Yes, he had heard of the famous M. Cambon. He had read about him in the *Police Gazette*, but he did not know him from Adam. So this explained things? This was why he had accompanied Mr. Dacre? Ah, the fellow must be speaking the truth. Perhaps he had better omit the apology.

"A blithering idiot?" he repeated. "How do you make that out? I saw the airplane. It buzzed round me seventeen times. It nearly made me sick, and then I saw what happened. The pilot pushed the girl from his machine, and her body fell towards the earth, landing on top of that hayrick. That's evidence, sir. Real evidence!" P.C. Gutteridge was in a complex state. He was both dignified and hurt. This was no way to treat a Crown witness.

M. Cambon broke into a grin.

"My priceless fool," he said, "you have only made matters worse. You say you saw an airplane, that it buzzed round you seventeen times, that it made you sick. Just so. It did make you sick, Gutteridge. It made you damned sick. It made you queer in the head. It made you see things. Your imagination got to work—because you were devilish sick—and you thought you saw that body fall from the machine. You fancied you saw it land on top of the hayrick. But that was all moonshine. You might as well have imagined you saw the airplane land on the hayrick. Now let me tell you something that has not occurred to you. Perhaps there was a murdered body on the hayrick. That is why you are lucky with your cock-and-bull story. Gutteridge, I advise you to go in for slimming. Your girth won't stand the strain of your terrific imagination!"

P.C. Gutteridge could have said a lot. But he knew M. Cambon was an important individual—one of the elect, like Dacre—and it would never do to offend him. It would be bad taste if he said what he thought of all Frenchmen. No, he had better keep his mouth shut. Wait until the case was tried in Court! When it came before the Judge of the Assize, when he, Gutteridge, was a Crown witness, then M. Cambon would look foolish.

"So you think it was imagination!" he jeered. "You think I ought to be put away, Monsieur Cambon, that I am a fit applicant for a lunatic asylum? In your eyes, I am nothing but a priceless fool, eh? Well, if that is so, I am not the only fool in Cottingdale. The Chief Constable has believed my story. He has never doubted me for an instant."

"Then the Chief Constable is in the same category," was the swift retort. "It means two idiots instead of one. Now, look here, Gutteridge. If you take my advice, you will tell those reporters a new version. You will make it plain, next time, that the air-pilot got on your nerves, that he affected your thinking-machine, that he made you see things that did not really happen. That is the only way to save your reputation, for believe me, P.C. Gutteridge, a ghastly murder of this kind is not committed in an airplane. On a hayrick—perhaps! In an airplane—no!"

With that parting shot, that left the constable speechless, he turned and entered the sitting-room. Dacre was still busy, yet he had heard every word. Most of it he put down to Cambon's peculiar temperament—he knew him of old—but he was a bit nettled all the same. Hang it all, that was no way to treat the honest Gutteridge. After all, a dastardly crime could be committed anywhere, even in a balloon, and there was no reason to think Gutteridge was fooling. Finding the body on the hayrick was grim reality, and Gutteridge did not spend Saturday afternoons on top of hayricks . . . At least he hoped not.

"Well, how is the great sleuth progressing?" Cambon asked satirically, as he re-entered. "I was trying to drive sense into that fool Gutteridge, but, like a priceless ass, and like all your English police, he's as obstinate as a mule. He still clings to the absurd notion that he saw the girl flung from the airplane. Wonder what he had for lunch? Perhaps he's a dope maniac! . . . Come, let's have a look, Dacre. Let me see this ghastly knife-wound with my own eyes!"

Dacre rose from the sofa, and the Frenchman took his place on the ground. He withdrew his own scientific instruments from an inner pocket, and, in the most detached fashion, examined the dead body. Like Dacre, he scrutinised the knife-wound with a long survey, almost with the methodical care of a surgeon, noting the ragged nature of the wound and the marks of the human teeth. Then he stared at the girl's features—a remarkably plain face—at the clothes she wore, at the brown shoes. Then he rose and turned to his colleague. He did not speak at once.

Dacre flashed him another peculiar glance.

"What is your verdict?" he asked.

He had made his own deduction, his own personal analysis; he had formed his own conclusion, he had noted everything important and relevant. Now he wanted to hear the opinion of the famous French expert.

After all, M. Cambon showed little sentiment. He was too much of a realist. All French detectives are trained in that hard school.

"Well, a peculiar kind of knife was used," he said slowly. "I doubt very much, Dacre, if you could find one like it on this side. If so, it has been brought from Southern Europe. It was, I venture to say, a dagger used by the Italian Fascisti, a derelict descendant of the famous Camorra band, one with a terribly ragged edge. A single thrust was sufficient. Death was instantaneous."

Dacre leaned forward. He pointed towards the wound.

"And the teeth?"

M. Cambon shrugged his shoulders.

"That presents a more sinister aspect. The inference is that the murderer, drank the blood of his victim, or performed some ghoulish act of that kind. It is all very bestial, but we are not concerned with that part of it. Your first job, Dacre, is to establish identity. That, after all, should be a simple matter. The poor girl has been photographed *ad nauseam*. By to-morrow every paper will have her portrait; by Monday she will be identified. That will mean the turn of the tide. Until then, you can do nothing."

Dacre gave a slow nod. That reasoning was parallel with his own. When he glanced at Cambon, he saw the French expert had been talking mechanically. He stared at the corpse in detached fashion. He was interested merely from the scientific side. The luminosity had disappeared from his blue eyes. His face was a trifle pale. He seemed in a kind of dream. Dacre wondered what he was thinking! Had a new inspiration occurred to Cambon?

"So far, I agree," Dacre said quietly. "Gutteridge, for the moment, is unimportant. He can add nothing to what he told the newspaper men, but I will have a few words with him later. The next move is to get hold of Dr. Gibbs. He should be here any moment. What a pity, Cambon, there is no clue or pointer. That dress contains no pocket. There are no concealed letters, no love epistles, no documents of any kind. Now with a man it would have been different. His letter-case would have told us everything. But women are so mysterious. And they are all alike—baffling, elusive, treacherous."

M. Cambon made a cold grimace.

"Ah, this type had few secrets," he ventured. "In Paris, we have thousands of her kind. This is no La Gioconda. Just the quiet, hard-working type of milliner, unaccustomed to recognition, unused to luxury, unacquainted with evil. Yet, despite all that—or was it because of it?—she was taken for a joy-ride by some devil in the guise of an air-pilot . . . *Tiens*, that story I do not swallow, Dacre. *Parblieu*, it is absurd, monstrous, illogical . . . More likely a motor-ride, then a quarrel, a sudden blaze of passion, the knife!"

Dacre stared hard at his colleague.

"M. Cambon," he protested, "I do not follow. It beats me why you are so incredible. To me, the airplane story is logical. And as for Gutteridge, I fear you do him a big injustice. I had a keen glance at him as I entered. No imagination there, my dear chap. Nothing but a loyal, methodical policeman, anxious to do his duty at all cost. He has told the truth. I am prepared to believe him. Nay, I do believe him. Gibbs will confirm whether he is right. He can tell us about the body, whether it has fallen from a height. That we must have confirmed!"

Cambon gave a dry laugh.

He twirled his dark moustache.

"Have it your own way," he answered. "But if my observation counts, Dacre, I fancy a pilot in mid-air—well, at four thousand feet—would have something else to think about than a ghoulish murder of this sort. I am a realist. That is why the Gutteridge story leaves me cold . . . Hello, who have we here?"

He turned and glared at the new-comer.

It was Dr. Gibbs, followed by Muir, the Chief Constable.

"Here he is, Mr. Dacre!" Muir exclaimed. "Report and everything written out. Gibbs, allow me to explain why Cottingdale is honoured this evening!"

A swift introduction followed, the Frenchman staring at the new-comer suspiciously. But Dacre followed convention, shook hands formally, and glanced at the report.

"This is what I want," he said quietly. "But, doctor, just let us have your views on one point. My colleague here is sceptical about the airplane. He thinks it too absurd, just a freakish kink in the brain of Gutteridge. May I ask what your examination revealed? Have you convinced yourself that this girl was flung from some tremendous height?"

Gibbs glared back at the Frenchman. He never liked foreigners, and Cambon irritated him. So devilish superior. As regards the murder, he treated that lightly. Murders were not a daily occurrence at Cottingdale, yet he was familiar with death, and he had satisfied himself that Gutteridge was right.

"Let me explain," he said quickly. "When I came upon the scene, I was inclined to think that Gutteridge had been drinking, or had gone suddenly loopy. Indeed, I told him so to his face. But, gentlemen, I have made an apology for my mistake. P.C. Gutteridge spoke the truth this afternoon. That girl, Mr. Dacre, was flung from a great height. If you want facts, let me inform you that her left leg is broken in two places, that part of the back is dislocated, and the hayrick alone saved the body from being crushed out of recognition. There are other signs as well, all clearly indicating that the girl received a terrific fall. I have not the slightest doubt about the Gutteridge version. I think the Home Office owes him a great debt."

"Ah, that is just the point," M. Cambon intervened. "If the Gutteridge version is correct, why has his story not been corroborated? That airplane was not built and designed for his delectation. I understand there was a cricket match in progress—the papers said so at least—then why did some other witness not come forward? Why was the story not confirmed? Come, a plain answer to a straight question, my dear Gibbs!"

The doctor blew his nose vigorously.

He confessed he was nonplussed.

Even the Chief Constable coughed. There was certainly that aspect.

Then Dacre came to the rescue.

"Let us be fair to Gutteridge," he appealed. "In other words, let us note three points. An airplane flying overhead does not create a sensation to-day, not even in remote Cottingdale, which I hardly knew was on the map! Secondly, think what a cricket duel meant between Ferndale and Cottingdale! Those spectators had only eyes for the game. Finally, even if one or two did suspect something wrong, or actually saw something fall from the machine, you must remember bad news travels fast, and a civilian, even in Cottingdale, is not over-anxious to be a Crown witness. Doubtless, when a few days have passed, or when the Yard asks other people to come forward, we may get a surprise,

M. Cambon. Until then, having heard the medical testimony, I suggest we allow the Gutteridge version to stand."

Cambon saw he had misfired. He switched the talk on another line.

"Let's glance at the hayrick," he suggested. "I want to see the position of it, and, incidentally, Gibbs, you might point out where that cricket match took place."

He seemed in a tremendous hurry to leave the room, but Dacre agreed to the proposal. As they left the farm, the latter was buttonholed by three Fleet Street men. To each he gave a short paragraph for their papers, only a few brief lines, but they were infinitely grateful. He asked them to say as little as possible, and he got rid of them with remarkable dexterity. But then Dacre was noted for his tact. Besides, it pays to be courteous to newspaper men.

The large crowd of morbid people still hung about the farm, but the constables soon cleared the path, and eventually the hayrick was reached. The ladder still rested against the side, and Dacre was the first man to ascend. He jumped lightly on top of the crushed hay, then luck favoured him for once. His right foot dislodged something. In a flash he picked it up. Only M. Cambon noticed the incident. He saw the swift movement of Dacre's hand to his pocket, bit his lip ruefully, but made no remark of any kind. Perhaps later, in the quietude of the Weymouth hotel, his rival would disgorge his clue. Dacre he knew from experience. A definite pointer was almost sacred.

When they reached the top of the hayrick Muir demonstrated his topography.

"There you are, gentlemen," he said forcibly, "about a mile distant, on my extreme left, the cricket field where Cottingdale played Ferndale this afternoon. And, according to the direction given by Gutteridge, that is the part of the sky—up there on my right—where the machine parted with its human freight. Hardly discernible, perhaps, to the players on the field—especially if it was the tea interval—but, of course, within the radius of anyone near this field."

Dacre hardly seemed listening. He was down on his hands and knees, searching furtively for some further clue, but the search eluded him, and he rose again to his feet.

"Look here," M. Cambon suddenly burst out, "we do look a lot of damned sheep standing here! Dacre, let me ask you a question, and it has nothing to do with murder. You are ravenously hungry, and I am dying for a drink. Are you going to remain here all night—on top of this hayrick—or do you come back with me to Weymouth? There can be no further developments until that girl is identified, and they can easily get hold of you by phone. Chief Constable Muir will keep you in immediate contact. What say you?"

They descended the ladder in single file. When they reached *terra firma*, Dacre turned to the French expert.

"Cambon," he said grimly, "I am sorry to send you back alone—very sorry indeed—but I intend to remain in Cottingdale!"

CHAPTER IV

A TERRIBLE PROPHECY

IF GENIUS was attributed to Dacre, he only smiled. He knew vastly different. There might be a modicum of intelligence, but the rest was hard work. Once started on a case, Dacre was the most industrious man in England. He had tireless energy, and until he roped in the individual he sought, or secured proof of guilt, he left self out of the question.

When M. Cambon returned that evening to Weymouth, Dacre got busy. He had a long interview with Gutteridge, during which he tried to get further data, particularly about the airplane and type of engine, but he had to confess failure in that respect. To Gutteridge it seemed an ordinary airplane, with nothing remarkable about it except it buzzed round him seventeen times, giving him that dizzy feeling in the head and the pain in his "little Mary," but apart from that he could add little to the report published.

Afterwards Dacre secured rooms in the "White Hart" Hotel, which is the most exclusive in Cottingdale. At any rate, it possessed a telephone, and before ordering dinner or worrying about himself at all, he got into communication with the Air Force in London.

Soon he was talking to an important Whitehall official. He explained he was not trying to buy an airplane, or even asking for a "joy-ride," but he wanted to know if any Government machine was over the Cottingdale area that afternoon, and, if so, full particulars concerning it. When the official heard his name, he came to earth with a bump and promised all the help in his power. Dacre then got in touch with Croydon, followed the same line of inquiry, and had precisely the same result. Everyone promised to do something.

That was quite what he expected, but when the thing would be done was quite a different point.

Then, still trusting in the goodness of humanity, he asked the Yard to get in touch with airplane clubs, and let him have a report before midnight. He rang up the Aerodrome at Filton, Bristol, also the Wessex Flying Club and confessed that everyone was tumbling over each other to help, but still no news about a machine over the Cottingdale district. It was like looking for an ostrich in a forest of monkeys! In addition to flying clubs, Dacre realised there were many airplanes privately owned, and that meant a separate line of investigation. It would take more time and patience; as there was no connecting link between them, but he switched the Yard over on that also, and was informed that the big London editors were trying to help. He was gratified at that last bit of news, for publicity he desired at all cost, and if there was any maniac going about in an airplane the sooner he was brought to earth the better. The Yard told him an appeal was broadcast for other witnesses to come forward.

When all this shouting through the telephone came to an end, Dacre hung up the receiver with a feeling his stomach was empty. It was ten o'clock, and the thought of food appealed to him at last. This terrific dilemma he explained to the manager of the "White Hart" Hotel, who buzzed round him in the same manner as Gutteridge's airplane, and in a few seconds he was led to the dining-room on the ground floor. It must have been a tremendously select place, because Dacre was the only diner to put in an appearance. It was here also that the head waiter proved to him that food could be obtained.

It was a trifle late for dinner, but a most excellent supper was prepared, and Dacre realised that even Cottingdale might have its compensations. True, it was nothing like the Ritz, Savoy, or Regal, but the items were excellent, and there was no fault with the wine or sweets. When he lit a Turkish cigarette at the end of the meal, Dacre was thankful the dining-room was empty, for he wanted to do some private thinking.

He saw the blinds were lowered, and that a cheerful fire burned in the grate.

Had he desired he could have retired to his own room, but there he might have missed this wonderful fire, and he was taking no chances. There was something about a fire that always appealed to him. It encouraged thought for one thing, and, after all, to have the capacity to think was sublime.

Dacre commenced to think hard.

Those thoughts of his were revolving round one object, and after three minutes he drew it from his waistcoat pocket. He stared at it with the gaze of an Oriental. It was the complete half of a broken gold bangle. That was what he picked up on the hayrick. It belonged to the murdered girl, because he had seen the other bangle on her right wrist, and had noted that the left bangle was missing. He made that observation in Jackson's farm-house, when engaged in the first survey of the body, and when he picked up the broken half on the hayrick, he knew it was his first clue.

Where was the other half?

Dacre gave a shrug.

Heaven knew the answer to that. But then Fate often played into his hand, and time and again he had been taught there was Providence. Perhaps, in some mysterious way, that other half would come into his possession.

If it did, he would recognise it.

How?

That was his secret.

Obeying some professional instinct, Dacre kept his find to himself, although there might be only a chance in a million of linking up his clue. Nevertheless, he could keep his mouth shut, and even if Cambon asked what he picked up, he would have given an enigmatic reply.

But the French expert knew the value of reticence, and, for a reason best known to himself, he did not refer to the matter. When he left Dacre, he extended him an invitation to Claridge's Hotel, but there was no guarantee he would stay in Weymouth. Two days might see him in Paris, or even in Switzerland. He was on holiday, therefore a bird of passage.

But he promised to maintain an interest in the case, and made Muir smile by saying he would pray for Gutteridge!

Then Dacre was called to the telephone.

It was Chief Constable Muir, and he rang through from Cottingdale Police Station. No, he had not found the airplane, nor the pilot, nor anything else. He just wanted to say there had been a development. A man named Robert Henderson had travelled up from Weymouth, and the murdered girl was his daughter. So he said at least. He had recognised the photograph in the papers, after returning from a neighbouring town, and had caught the first train to Cottingdale. To make certain, Muir had taken him to Jackson's farm, then back to the station to make a deposition, and at the station he remained. He was a widower, and there was no doubt the victim was his daughter. He was in a terrible state of grief. Could Mr. Dacre come at once?

Mr. Dacre could.

Mr. Dacre reached Cottingdale Police Station in three minutes, and Muir awaited him in his private office. Inspector Frank Murray was there also, and in a room adjoining in case he was required, was the immortal P.C. Gutteridge.

"So identity has been established?" Dacre asked the question swiftly. The Inspector took his hat and coat, and the expert subsided in the nearest chair. In a case of this kind, identity was a tremendous factor. On it would hinge all the big developments.

"Completely established!" answered Chief Constable Muir. He rubbed his hands in invisible soap; he was manifestly pleased. "Naturally the father is in an awful state, but we thought it better to phone you. I presume, Mr. Dacre, you will question him without delay. We have got him in that room with P.C. Gutteridge, who, with wonderful presence of mind, has given him a nip of brandy, and I think he might be ready. We have told him all about you in advance, Mr. Dacre, and he is grateful you have taken up the case. Would you like to see him alone, or will you talk to him in our presence?"

Dacre nodded.

"No need to run away!" he said forcibly. "I am simply going to ask a few questions, and the Inspector can jot down the words as I go along. I don't think it will be necessary for Henderson to sign a statement, not unless he can give us testimony about the air-pilot. Show him in, Muir, and let us see what advance we can make."

The Inspector left the room at once, retired to the adjoining apartment, then returned with an elderly man obviously overcome with grief. He wore a dark-grey, ill-fitting suit, with cloth cap to match, and badly-made boots. He had thin, pinched features, as if life presented a terrific puzzle, and the brown eyes showed his distress.

He gave a sob as he entered, but the Inspector led him to a chair, and Dacre was introduced.

"God bless you, sir, for coming down!" he exclaimed in a broken voice. "I have read about you many times, Mr. Dacre, and I know you are the best they have got at the Yard. The shock of this murder, sir—it has nearly killed me. I can't realise—I can't believe that Ruth is dead!"

He commenced sobbing afresh, and Dacre waited for him to regain control. He spoke gently in the interval.

"It's a terrible business!" he said sympathetically. "An awful crime, Mr. Henderson, but we are going to get the man who did it. That is why I have been sent from the Yard. Now, when you have pulled yourself together, I want you to tell me everything about your daughter. That is the only way we can advance. If you will just answer my questions, that may give me the information I want. First of all, your address in Weymouth?"

Henderson took off his cap. He placed it on his knee.

"I am a painter by trade, sir," he replied. "My little business is at 3 Moorgate Street, Weymouth. It's only three minutes' walk from the pier. You can't miss it!"

The Inspector wrote every word down. The Chief Constable leaned back. He was trying to smoke a cigarette, but it was really to hide his feelings. He was a kind-hearted man, and the sight of Henderson's grief appalled him.

"And this joy-ride on the airplane?" Dacre pursued. "Know anything about it?"

Henderson held up his hands in horror.

"I was never more amazed in my life!" he gasped. "Ruth is my only daughter. She is twenty-three years of age, and never was there a more quiet or respectable girl. For two years she has worked in a Weymouth boot factory, but lately she has been on short time, and this week she finished on Wednesday. She has been going to pictures like other girls, but I never knew she met anyone in particular. I never heard about any air-pilot, so if an acquaintance was struck up, Ruth kept very quiet about it. She knew, of course, I would never allow her to go off with a stranger, so I suppose that was why she did not speak. But you could have knocked me down with a feather when I heard she had been in a flying machine!"

Dacre nodded afresh.

"So you knew nothing about the flying business?"

"Nothing whatever, sir!"

"And you never saw her in company with a member of the Air Force, or heard about her being seen with an air-pilot?"

"Never once, sir!"

The Inspector wrote that down.

"And now, Mr. Henderson, I want your full confidence," Dacre continued. "Remember, you must conceal nothing. As far as I understand character, your daughter was a straight, God-fearing girl. That is the impression she has given me—even in death! You can therefore understand that we are all anxious to help, all determined to hunt down the brute who committed this terrible crime. If we are to do that, you must keep nothing back. My next question is straightforward. Was your daughter engaged, or keeping company with any young man?"

Henderson replied without hesitation.

"Not for the past year, sir. She broke off her engagement with Ted Wilkinson, the postman, and since then kept much to herself. She had one young girl friend named Mary

Brookes. She lives at 19 Harcourt Street, Weymouth, and she will tell you the same thing. Mary and Ruth went about a lot together. I don't think they were interested in young men, sir. They seemed to enjoy themselves more on their own, and there has been so much unemployment in Weymouth, I think all idea of settling down is knocked out of their heads."

The Inspector was a good shorthand writer. He had everything down in black and white.

"Now what about letters?" Dacre asked thoughtfully. "Has any strange man sent love-letters to your daughter, or tried to create a friendly feeling through the post?"

Henderson shook his head.

"Nothing like that, sir!" he replied. "My daughter was a good girl. I don't think for one moment she would have carried on a clandestine correspondence."

"She was interested in air-machines?"

"Nothing out of the ordinary. I did hear her remark now and again, she would like a flip in a plane, just like any other girl, I suppose—and that is just what must have happened. When my back was turned, she must have met some scoundrel, when she was shopping this morning, or she may have run across him last night, or one day during the week, and the fatal appointment was made. But why Ruth should have been murdered beats me hollow. Perhaps he wanted her to fly to Paris, or to some place where she did not like, and when she refused, he must have behaved like a lunatic!"

Dacre gave a comprehensive nod.

"It must have been something like that," he admitted. "Well, Henderson, what time did you leave home this morning, and when did you get back to Weymouth?"

"I had a little job across in Portland. That's not far from Weymouth, Mr. Dacre, but it meant leaving home after breakfast—about nine in the morning, I believe—and I did not get back until six o'clock to-night. God help me, I shall never forget this day as long as I live . . . The Portland job kept me till five o'clock, Mr. Dacre, then I had tea with a friend, and that took another twenty minutes!"

"And when did you see the paper?"

"Not till I came back, sir. To tell the truth, it was a neighbour came running in with it. An old friend of the family, Mrs. Hepburn by name, and she said to me: 'Where is Ruth?' I said: 'I don't know. Gone to the pictures with Mary Brookes, I expect. 'That's her usual programme!' Then she showed me the paper—all trembling like—and when I saw the photo I almost collapsed!"

Dacre thanked him for the information. The interview was at an end.

"We will let you know about the inquest," he said in a kind voice. "You must have time to arrange about the funeral. I will see the body is sent down to Weymouth, Mr. Henderson. It won't cost you a penny. And if you hear any further news—especially about an air-pilot speaking to any girls in Weymouth—get in touch with me at once!"

"That I will, sir!" promised the sobbing man. He rose heavily to his feet. He seemed bowed down with the weight of years.

"No need for you to return to-night!" interposed the Chief Constable. "We can soon find room for you in Cottingdale, Mr. Henderson. Leave that with me, and we will fix you up in ten minutes. What do you say?"

Henderson squared his shoulders. He shook his head in determined fashion.

"No, I must get back home to-night!" he declared fiercely. "I am going to make enquiries. I am going to ask all Ruth's friends, and specially that Mary Brookes, if my daughter was ever seen with an Air Force man, or with an air-pilot of any kind; and, if so, I will get full particulars. You will hear from me again, Mr. Dacre. I'm going to help as much as I can—and if ever I get that hell-hound who killed my daughter—Well, God have mercy on his soul, for I won't!"

He passed out of the room in the company of Inspector Murray, and when he had gone there was a curious silence. Dacre was thinking hard. Then he turned and glanced at the Chief Constable.

"Say, Muir, you are perfectly certain there is no aerodrome near Weymouth?"

The Chief Constable was positive.

"That I have already verified," he said quickly. "The nearest aerodrome of any importance is Bristol. But, of course, a pilot could come as readily from Croydon or Farnborough, or even the East Coast. Besides, it may be a privately-owned machine, and then Heaven help us in the search. They are as plentiful now as gooseberries!"

"Quite," Dacre assented. "Well, I have got the Yard busy on the flying clubs, Muir, and it is up to you to make what enquiries you can. As regards the privately-owned machines, try and get me a detailed report of all in the Cottingdale district, or indeed within the county. The inquest, I think, we will fix for Monday at three, but I will confirm that later. Thank you for ringing me up about Henderson. On the surface, we may not seem to have obtained much information, yet he has led us to the town of Weymouth, and I will pursue close investigations in that area."

Muir rose and accompanied him to the door.

It was a moonlit night, and Cottingdale was bathed in a wonderful silence. The air was calm and still, but to these two men it breathed an overpowering sense of tragedy. The crime of that murdered girl was vivid in their minds.

"Very good, Mr. Dacre," Muir rejoined. "And how do you find things at the 'White Hart'? Comfortable, I trust. I gave the manager special instructions about you, and if there is any complaint about the food, just let me know!"

"I am very comfortable, thanks!" the expert said gratefully. "Much obliged, Muir, for your kindness. The manager is a good fellow, only he thinks I am going to stay two months, and soon he will be disillusioned. You see, my friend, I am a bit of a fatalist, and sometimes I glance into the future without gazing at a crystal. I have an idea these airplane horrors have only commenced. I hope I am wrong, but do not be surprised if, within forty-eight hours, there is another tragedy!"

It was like a bolt from the blue.

Muir was staggered. He stepped back aghast.

"My God!" he said in a dramatic whisper. "Surely not, Dacre. Surely not?"

"I feel it in my bones!" was the prophetic rejoinder. "And by the way, Muir, there is an old saying at the Yard that a murderer returns to gaze upon the scene of the crime. That is often true. You might ask your men to keep a good look-out during the next few days, and if an airplane is spotted in the Cottingdale district, make every effort to get full particulars. Let them ferret out from what direction it has come, and try and get in touch with me at once. Many of these flying clubs are in touch with the machines by wireless, and you will find Croydon, Bristol, and London only too ready to help!"

The Chief Constable gave his solemn promise.

"I take it, Mr. Dacre, you want full particulars in each case?"

"Yes, as much detail as possible. That does not mean we are going to land on the pilot who came here this afternoon, but these air people are mostly acquainted with each other, and a chance remark may work wonders so far as I am concerned. We only desire a pointer—and the rest I am content to leave with Providence!"

CHAPTER V

DACRE HAS A VISITOR!

DACRE was in for a surprise. He got back to the "White Hart" about ten-thirty that evening, and found the manager awaiting him with considerable impatience. It appeared there was a young lady in the supper-room, and she was very anxious to meet the Yard expert.

"Who is she?" Dacre asked swiftly.

"I believe the name is Lena Somerton," the manager said promptly. "She has booked a room here for to-night, but her handwriting is almost illegible. She is having some supper in that room you have just vacated, and she wants to see you the moment you arrive. A very interesting personality, Mr. Dacre, but she brought only a suit-case, and I am always inclined to be suspicious. She entered the hotel half an hour ago!"

Dacre smiled. He would see this young lady with the interesting personality. He gave his hat and coat to an attendant, paused to light a cigarette, and made his way to the supper-room. It was the apartment containing the large fire, and in any case he intended returning to it.

But he was not prepared for the vision that met his gaze.

A young lady sat at the table within comfortable distance of the fire. Apparently the supper had just come to an end. When she looked up at Dacre, he was struck by the magic of her eyes. They were blue, large, and lustrous, and flashed with a dare-devil courage that appealed. There was something attractive about that lovely face, something fascinating about the clear, transparent skin, the high forehead that spoke of intellect and determination. The mouth was small and mobile, the figure singularly graceful, the clothes of remarkably good taste. The brown dress suited her to perfection.

"Hillo, Dacre," she said coolly, "where have you been all this time? I have been waiting thirty minutes!"

The expert was staggered. All women to him were anathema, because he knew their sex well, but this one was different—vastly different. There was something intriguing about her that magnetised, that made him wish to dominate, that taunted him with a feeling of calm superiority. He knew he was antagonised at that moment, yet the drawing power was greater. He was more interested than he cared to confess.

"I am very much obliged to you for waiting," he said courteously, "but I am afraid you have me at a disadvantage. Won't you tell me your name and all about yourself?"

She smiled.

"I won't tell you a lot," she said in the same cool voice, "but you can have a few of the crumbs. I'm Lena Somerton, attached to the *Evening Sentinel*, and sent down from Fleet Street to worry you to death. In other words, I have been commissioned by the owner and editor of the paper to get all the facts about the Cottingdale murder, and not to let you leave my sight a moment. That is going to suit me down to the ground, for if I can get a scoop for the *Sentinel* there is a big chance of my promotion. Are you willing to help?"

"That all depends," Dacre observed, throwing himself into an easy chair. It was close to the fire, and from that angle he surveyed this enterprising lady-journalist. He had heard of these creatures but was never quite certain they existed. He was more impressed than ever by her loveliness, but he kept that fact to himself.

"Now you are talking Greek!" she ventured. "Please say on what your help depends?" She was in the act of finishing the last meal of the day, and the glance she flung at Dacre was full of courage. This was no milk-sop girl sent down to be fooled. This Lena Somerton was shrewd, capable, and determined, and ready to prove that in any given emergency.

"Oh, several things," he answered. "In the first place, I am not quite sure whether I am interested in the *Sentinel*. I hate the paper like poison, I detest both the editor and the owner, and I do not see why I should render you any assistance. What claim do you think you might have?"

Lena Somerton wiped her dress with a handkerchief, then selected the chair opposite.

"I think you are dreadfully absurd," she replied. "Of one thing you may be positive, Mr. Dacre. I'm not interested one little bit in you, except in a journalistic sense, so we had better understand that from the beginning."

Dacre expressed himself in a loud laugh.

"You can take it from me that you are perfectly safe," he observed ironically. "I belong to the Noble Order of Women-Haters, and I don't intend to make any exception. Sorry to be so downright blunt, Miss Somerton, but I think you asked for it!"

She gave a little discreet nod, but not a smile disturbed her features.

"Your reputation in that respect has reached Fleet Street," she continued, "so there is no need to apologise. But in case you might be tempted to change your mind, Mr. Dacre, please let me inform you that I am a High-Priestess of the Noble Order of Man-Haters. So you can take it from me that you are perfectly safe!"

Dacre felt tickled to death. Not since a famous horse had crossed her legs on the racecourse had he been so infinitely amused. He held out his cigarette case, and she extracted one with an air of absolute equality. She even struck a match and lit Dacre's cigarette before applying it to her own.

"Having exchanged those pleasant preliminaries," he ventured, "I suppose there is a possibility we may co-exist. I am not sure if you will care for that brand of cigarette. It happens to be Turkish, but I think you can depend on the mild flavour."

"I simply adore Turkish cigarettes," she confessed. "That seems to be the only point we have in common."

As she spoke, she gave him another glance of keen scrutiny. This was the first time she had met the famous detective, and as a journalist her glance was critical. She was glad to read honesty in his dark glowing eyes, and that trick of bringing his lips together made her realise he was a determined personage. That was all in his favour. He also conveyed an impression that he was genuinely modest, and that appealed to her most of all. But such approval she would keep rigorously to herself. She could never afford to admit that this Yard man had won her admiration.

"So you are Malcolm Dacre!" she said softly. "Dear me, I have read all your terrible adventures in our paper, but I never thought I would be destined to go on your trail. Now that reminds me about the journalistic side. We have got all the stuff you transmitted to the Press Association, but we hear a man has come up to see you from Weymouth, and that he has communicated with the Cottingdale Police. Can you put me wise on that?"

There was a delightful brightness about her eyes. There was also a subtle sense of the perfume she need. Finally, there was just the faintest tinge of colour in those lovely cheeks. He gave a brief nod.

"That man was the father of the murdered girl," he informed her. "His name is Robert Henderson, and he lives at 3 Moorgate Street, Weymouth. He recognised the photo in the paper, and came up here to the Cottingdale Police Station. Now after identifying his daughter he has gone back to Weymouth. The girl's name is Ruth Henderson. She was employed in a Weymouth boot factory."

A little notebook appeared on her knee. She wrote everything down.

"Go on!" she said breathlessly. "Tell me a lot more, Dacre. Surely you have made some new point of contact? Surely Henderson was able to give you some facts about the air-pilot?"

"Absolutely none. That is just where I have been disappointed. But we are glad that identity has been established. The father appears to have been kept in the dark. He says his daughter had no great interest in airplanes, and had never, to the best of his knowledge, been up in a machine. She kept company with a young girl named Mary Brookes, who resides at 19 Harcourt Street, Weymouth, and she may throw some further light on the affair. The father never heard of any air-pilot. He had to make a journey to Portland this morning, and concludes the meeting may have taken place in his absence. Failing that, he thinks the appointment may have been made during the week."

Lena jotted down the name and address of the girl Brookes, wrote a few more lines, then glanced at the expert.

"You are not such a terrible monster after all," she confessed. "Those few pars. will prove to the editor that I am doing something. But say, what about love letters—?"

"I mentioned that, but Henderson would have none of it. He declares his daughter never kept up a clandestine correspondence, and I believe he is right in that respect. The dead girl does not seem that type. She appears to be an innocent victim of some ghoulish devil—!"

Lena leaned forward.

"That hardly fits in with your hatred of my sex!" she protested. "But if that vampire business is true, Dacre, you must leave no stone unturned in getting on the track of that fiend. I want to help all I possibly can. I have been sent down on this job, and I won't rest until the murderer is landed. Every titbit of gossip I can find, every scrap of information about air-machines, will be brought straight to you. I will promise you that much. The brute who knifed that girl must be caught!"

Dacre sent a cloud of smoke to the ceiling.

"I hope you won't think me frightfully rude," he said, "but does all this come within your job? I mean—you almost suggest you are going to employ the tactics of a lady detective"

"I don't think you rude for asking a perfectly straight question," she conceded. "Perhaps I had better let you into a State secret. You see, Mr. Malcolm Dacre, I was specially selected for this work because I happen to have qualified as an air-pilot. I belong to a club outside London, and hold my flying licence in case of National emergency. As I know a good many flying people, and everything that is to be known about an air-bus, it was thought my special knowledge might count."

Dacre concealed his surprise. This girl was more efficient than he thought. She was prepared to venture up alone in an airplane, and had managed to secure her ticket as a pilot. Yes, Lena Somerton was going to prove a useful adjunct, but it would never do to throw a bouquet right at her head.

"You certainly will be able to help," he admitted; "but although you have the ability to fly, Miss Somerton, I shall have to have proof that you possess tact. You see, my enquiries are being pursued over a wide area, with the Yard, the Air Force, and a lot of other people co-operating. I have even got in touch with private flying clubs, and arrangements are also being made to link up privately-owned machines. I am just wondering if it would be wise to let you move about as a freelance—!"

She gave him one contemptuous glance, then rose to her feet.

"I had an idea you would prove a mug," she said boldly. "But friend Dacre, whether you think it wise or otherwise, allow me to inform you I am a free agent. I was willing to co-operate to a certain extent, but if my information is not useful to you, then the editor of my paper may have other views. And remember that I have the power to criticise the Yard and all its members, and if I put you down as the greatest nincompoop that ever merited the name of sleuth-hound, then you will know who to blame. Meanwhile, I am going to ring up Fleet Street, and get this stuff over the line, after which I am going to take a small glass of brandy, and go straight to bed. Doubtless we shall meet in the pink and pearly future!"

Dacre stretched his legs and yawned.

"A wonderful piece of oratorical humbug," he remarked. "But incidentally, my good girl, do not be too proud of that air licence! You see, I happen to possess a ticket myself only I don't make a song about it!"

The girl bit her lip in vexation. The single spot of crimson on each cheek increased. A dangerous light entered the blue eyes.

"So you can handle a joy-stick!" she breathed. "How clever. Tell me, angel, where did you qualify, and who supplied the smelling salts?"

"I wangled my ticket at Northolt Aerodrome!" he said humbly.

She gave a little smile and left the room.

Dacre went on smoking for twenty minutes.

He took up a magazine and tried to read, but it was difficult to concentrate on anything but a girl's face. He realised that a disturbing influence had entered his life. No girl had ever fastened on his thoughts, no girl had changed his philosophy of life, but this girl seemed different to all the others. Lena Somerton was unique. She affected him in a manner that left him breathless.

She was the modern type *in excelsis*. There were no flies on her. She knew every corner of a man's mind, saw through his masculine vagaries, and seemed contemptuous of his whole sex. Into the bargain she had intelligence and resource. She was not afraid to come alone to the "White Hart" Hotel, or to treat him like an ordinary human. There was no gush about her. She was straight, practical, and sophisticated. Like himself she was absolutely sincere, and that was where they touched a common denominator.

Well, she would have to be kept in her place.

No Fleet Street woman-journalist was going to teach him his business, or poke her nose into it either.

Despite her cleverness, and the fact that she represented a leading London newspaper, she would have to be taught discretion. She had too much of the American temperament. If she imagined she was going to "bust-in" at every interview, or get the latest news about it, she was in for a disillusion. She would only get what news he allowed her to have, and if she sent anything through that was not approved, then he would show her there was such a thing as censorship.

Strange he wished to dominate her in this manner.

Already there was a struggle for the mastery.

How would that struggle end?

He was cogitating on that point when the door opened and she re-entered. It was a wonderful surprise. He thought she had retired for the evening.

"What has happened?" he gasped. "Have they drunk all the brandy?"

"Don't be a chump!" she begged. "I have never taken brandy in my life. I got through to Fleet Street and woke the editor up. He seemed at least to be half-asleep. He is delighted to know that I am going to teach you to catch murderers. By the way, you have got my magazine, and I came back specially for it. I have got the most tiresome habit of reading in bed, but that is because I possess a first-class brain!"

Dacre passed the magazine across with an apology.

"No idea you read rubbish of that kind," he said cynically. "What a nuisance you should worry me again! Would you like to know that I have thought of a plan to get rid of you?"

"Oh yeh!" she retorted, imitating the American twang. "But how do you know your plan will succeed?"

"Well, there is no harm in trying at least. May I ask if you have got a gun?"

"Sure thing!" she twanged again, and produced an automatic from some pocket of her dress. It appeared in a flash, and Dacre grinned softly. This girl could take care of herself. He saw it was something more than a toy, and that she knew how to use it.

In another flash it disappeared.

"Well, that is splendid!" he vouchsafed. "You see, it occurred to me that you might act the red herring. If this air-minded villain still patrols the vicinity of Weymouth, intent upon coaxing girls for joy-rides in his machine—and I believe that possibility exists—then you might take on the job of enchantress! That is, you could spread the tidings that you were keen on flying, that nothing would delight you more than a flip, and you only wished you could meet some air-pilot!"

The girl's eyes sparkled.

She advanced a few paces.

"But that would give me the most glorious thrill in my life," she replied. "I want the chance to run across that brute. I want to do something vital in this case. It will mean a splendid scoop for the paper, and I could lead the fiend into the nicest trap. Dacre, I believe you really have brains!"

"Possibly I have," he conceded, "but don't run away with the idea that I want you to do the whole thing. On no consideration must you enter his machine. Lead him a dance if you like, but when the chance offers get in touch with me by phone, and I will see if you can be rescued."

Lena looked at him squarely.

That dare-devil flush returned to her eyes.

"How positively kind you might be!" she sighed. "But look here, my woman-hater, I make no promises. If I see an opening to capture this brute myself, and with the aid of this little automatic, I might find no reason to trouble you by phone!"

She was teasing, of course.

"But that is hardly fair," he demurred. "Seeing I am giving you *carte blanche* in the matter, surely you are going to let me in on the grand climax?"

"I will give the matter my full consideration," she replied with the air of a Lady Mayoress. "But when do I start this new stunt?"

"As soon as you like. Frankly, I don't think much will be gained in Cottingdale. The arrival of Henderson from Weymouth has made matters more interesting in that district. If this fiend incarnate is still hovering round that seaside town, we had better make tracks there at once."

"Where do I find you?" she asked.

"In Claridge's Hotel, Weymouth. A friend of mine is staying there at present. I refer to M. Cambon, the distinguished member of the French *Sûreté*. He wanted me down there this evening, so I think I will accept his offer. When can you start?"

She slipped into a chair near the fire.

"I will go down there to-morrow," she said quietly. "Dacre, pardon me changing the subject. What made you a woman-hater?"

The expert grinned.

"Life!" he said tersely.

"Meaning you have been let down often—?"

"On the contrary, I have had little to do with your sex, Miss Somerton. But my experience at the Yard has been that of a realist. I have proved your kind to be treacherous in the extreme, to have only the faintest idea of loyalty, and to be falling over each other in the effort to subjugate men for your own amusement."

Lena coloured violently again.

She was making a big effort to keep from smiling.

"But how absurd," she exclaimed. "Why, you have got a most distorted view of my sisters, Dacre. We can hardly claim to be angels, you know, but we are not really all treacherous. I believe there are one or two exceptions. Have you never tried to find out?"

Dacre gave that hopeless shrug.

"That is what Life has taught me," he replied. "What has it taught you about men?"

"That you are all a pretty rotten lot, and that even the saintliest of your tribe could never be worthy to undo a woman's shoelace! The majority of you are so primitive, Dacre, that candidly I prefer dogs!"

"Do you speak from personal experience?"

"Yes, I've had a sample of one or two rotters, and they will do me for a lifetime. Still, they taught me a lesson, and that is the big point!"

The attendant entered to say that Dacre was wanted on the telephone. He rose at once.

It was the Chief ringing up from the Yard.

CHAPTER VI

A GHASTLY SIGHT

THE SUNDAY papers were full of the murder.

It was a crime that convulsed England, and there had been nothing like it for ten years.

Ruth Henderson, a respectable girl working in a Weymouth boot factory, had been met by a man and offered a joy-ride in an airplane. Some inducement led the girl to accept, and, without a word to her father or girl friend, she went with the pilot on that ill-fated venture. What happened would always be a mystery. But there was no doubt about the climax. The girl had been stabbed to death, and not content with the crime, the murderer had drank her life-blood: either the crime had been committed by a madman, or the fiend was not fit to live.

Then the body was flung from the machine. It hurtled through the air until it fell on, a hayrick, where a Cottingdale policeman observed the tragedy, and there was no attempt to hide the murder. There had been no such ghastly crime in air history, and every paper contained grim headlines about the outrage.

Thousands of newspaper readers shuddered, and all over England flying men commented on the crime. In the London Air Force Headquarters, in every provincial aerodrome, in all the flying clubs of Great Britain, this murder formed the one topic of conversation.

Everyone knew that Malcolm Dacre was engaged on the case, so every move of the famous detective was chronicled, and his photograph appeared in all the papers. Into the bargain, there was widespread desire to give Dacre every help, and this was proved by the countless messages to the Yard.

Similar messages reached Chief Constable Muir, and when it was known the inquest was fixed for Monday, a rumour circulated that there would be sensational developments. It was hinted that Malcolm Dacre had found a pointer, that there was every possibility of an arrest, and one paper went so far as to allege that a prominent member of the Air Ministry was concerned.

All these rumours were baseless, and after breakfast that Sunday morning, Dacre assured the Press Association that certain journalists were liars, that others suffered from a feverish imagination, and that the remainder should be painlessly exterminated. With his hand on his heart, he told them there were no developments of any kind, beyond the fact that identity had been established, and there was not the faintest suggestion of a pointer. When he finished, he thought he would like to send the Press Association to Hades as well, but on reflection he decided they might justify their existence.

Then his difficulties commenced.

After breakfast he met Lena Somerton in the coffee-room. Apparently she had finished her morning meal, although a trifle late in the process, but then girls always took a long time to dress, and no doubt lady journalists were in the same category. He would have to extend his forgiveness. Then he got a terrific shock, for in the full glory of morning sunlight, Lena burst upon his vision like an exotic dream. She was radiant with life, health, and happiness, and those lustre-blue eyes were filled with the same dare-devil courage. She had changed to a white travelling dress, and it fitted her like a glove. On her head was a dazzling red beret, and underneath the loveliest face in the world.

He drew a deep breath.

Was it possible such Evil could exist in the world!

"Well, Dacre, I have caught you!" she exclaimed. "You were going to sneak away from the hotel, and not give me the faintest intimation of your whereabouts. Surely you are not rushing off to Weymouth so early? I did not intend to go until after luncheon, for I want a special interview with the immortal Gutteridge, but if you are going to offer me a ride in your car, I am inclined to place my life in your hands."

Dacre thought of the worst word in the dictionary.

It eluded him. Then he invented a special swear word, but took care that he muttered it under his breath.

Although his dark eyes smiled, there was a quiet line round his lips.

"There has been a slight change in my programme," he informed her. "My Yard Chief rang up last night, and there was another phone message this morning. Reports have been coming in through the night, and one has caught my attention. It concerns a private airplane, to be found at a place called Mountdale, about seven miles from this hotel, and the man who owns it is known as Major Frank Hardy. I hear he is related to some peer of the realm, and is an individual of unlimited wealth. He is a widower who has travelled a lot, and is fifty-seven years of age. A little bird whispers that his plane was out yesterday, and he seems strangely non-communicative. I have made up my mind to pay him a call—it may not amount to anything at present—but there is a chance I may be favoured by the gods."

Lena Somerton gazed at him squarely.

A kiss-curl peeped from under the red beret.

She looked positively alluring.

"You mean that Hardy is a mystery?"

Dacre gave a slow nod.

"Neither the Yard nor the authorities know much about him," he confessed. "He took that house six months ago, and went there direct from the Continent. He lives with a housekeeper and one or two servants, whom he engaged when he arrived in England, but beyond that there is little data. Yet the tradespeople say his cheques are honoured, that he has turned Mountdale into a mansion, and that he is a very cultured gentleman. I wonder! Perhaps a talk with him will be useful."

Lena seemed pondering.

The blue eyes narrowed.

Never had she looked so adorable.

"You realise that distance is nothing to a plane?" she ventured. "This Major Hardy may be worth a visit if he is an enigma, but the man who committed that crime, Dacre, was a lot more shrewd than that. I don't imagine his machine is in the vicinity. For all we know, it may be lodged about the north of England, or on the South or East Coast, or it may even come from Wales. Do not think I am trying to grandmother you, but the point I am concentrating on is this: do I get invited on this trip to Mountdale, or would you rather leave your little Lena behind?"

Dacre muttered the same oath under his breath.

The girl wondered what it was, for she saw his lips move.

Then she laughed. How stupid men were! Fancy trying to deceive a woman!

"I would rather you went on to Weymouth," he declared. "That is the best plan I can think of getting rid of you, and when I see you at Claridge's Hotel, I may have something for you to phone Fleet Street. Meanwhile, I want you to keep this visit out of the papers. Nothing can be gained by publishing how many times I light a cigarette."

"Quite," Lena affirmed, "but as I did not contemplate going near Weymouth until this afternoon, I want to know why I should not accompany you to Mountdale? Supposing you fainted on the way? Supposing you found you could not drive the beastly car, or something like that? . . . Say, I may learn a lot more from Hardy as a journalist. Get the car and everything ready. I have made up my mind to go with you, and that is an end to it!"

Dacre swore three times in rapid succession.

Each time he swallowed hard.

How he hated all daughters of Eve at that moment!

Then he allowed himself another slow grin. Gradually it dawned on him that Lena Somerton was charming, that indeed she was the most attractive girl on earth, and that to refuse her anything was positively banal.

The two blue eyes were fixed on him. He groaned aloud.

"Can you drive a car?" he asked.

"Can I milk a goat?"

"Very well," he declared, "you can act as my chauffeur, and if you exceed the speed limit you will be summarily dismissed. Now get this in your ear. The Chief Constable has placed a car at my disposal. He is even allowing me free petrol, but I suppose I am responsible for damages. That car is in the hotel garage, and in two seconds it will be ready. If you want another small brandy, you had better hurry!"

"I will take a cocktail before lunch," she promised. "Until then, I am on the wagon."

Dacre turned to an hotel attendant and gave a swift order. In four minutes the car was waiting at the door.

The manager watched them depart with a knowing smile.

Poor fool, it seemed to him the beginning of a perfect Romance.

But then hotel managers are always soft-brained!

Yes, Lena proved she could drive. In case the reverse order of things proved correct, Dacre superintended her movements at the wheel. He pointed out the direction of the run, and again warned her about the speed limit. That was because the car was beginning to fly like a bird. Still, it was a glorious Sunday morning in August, with the sun bursting the hedgerows, and the whole world seemingly at Peace. There was a constant twitter of birds from the trees—somewhere aloft a lark trilled in ecstasy—and the wild flowers waved a welcome from neighbouring fields.

A golden silence fell between the pair.

They seemed to avoid each other's eyes.

The girl was thrilled for the first time in life.

It was a wonderful experience because she was unable to understand herself. She was conscious that antagonism existed between her and this man, that he remained remote and detached, that he was a perfectly insoluble puzzle. Yet it was like the moth and the candle. Dacre exercised a power that was irresistible and complete.

"Say," she observed in a low voice, "it's difficult to think of crime on a morning like this!" She turned as she spoke, and he saw her face aflame with some new-found happiness. That sudden light in her eyes gave him a shock.

Good heavens, what did it mean?

Was this girl falling in love with him?

Was that the paradox of it all?

Dacre cursed himself for making such a blunder. Why the devil had he permitted her to come with him? Was this his idea of keeping her in her place? Was this a demonstration of his profound hatred of the opposite sex? Why, she was more dangerous than he thought! Apparently her aim was to make him behave like a fool, then she would reprove him for indulging in flirtation. That was the way these creatures worked.

"I don't know," he muttered cynically. "I often wish to murder people, and if I had the artistic temperament, possibly I would select a day with the sun shining in the heavens. It all depends on whom I murder. Some people I know should be smothered in darkness."

"Don't be absurd," she whispered. "You never could murder anyone, Dacre. You are far too hyper-sensitive! You see, I have guessed that already. Didn't know, I suppose, that I was putting you under the analytical lens?"

Dacre gasped. So she was a psychologist as well! She had found out his hyper-sensitive state! What would she discover next?

"Take the second road on the left," he instructed, glancing at a small map on his knee, "and don't try to drive this car on two wheels. Remember I am a poor man, and I don't want a horrible accident!"

Lena drove on furiously for a few seconds.

Then she put the brake on and the car came to a full stop.

He turned and stared at her in amazement.

"What the devil's wrong?" he asked.

"Nothing," she answered. "I merely fancied the psychological moment had arrived. Aren't you going to kiss me, Dacre?"

The detective swallowed hard.

Not since Mussolini became Dictator had he received such a shock.

"Kiss you," he blurted back. "What the blazes put that idea in your head!" His tone could not have been more uncouth.

The girl laughed in grim fashion.

A crimson spot appeared on each cheek.

The blue eyes were luminous.

"I felt certain you would be making the effort at some part of the journey," she explained, "so I thought it better to get the rotten taste over. You see, when I was a child I always took my medicine before lunch . . . But is the idea so very obnoxious?"

She leaned just a trifle towards him—provokingly, daringly—and all the witchery of her beauty tempted.

But he moved away like a frightened schoolboy.

"Don't be a giddy fool," he said brutally. "Look here, Miss Somerton, I have something else to do than play the sentimental idiot. I have taken you on this jaunt with the understanding you were going to drive this car. If you can't play the game in that respect, then better let me take the wheel!"

That did it.

With a little toss of the head, Lena jumped into the road.

"That settles it," she said vigorously. "I'm going back. I have changed my mind. I think you are perfectly horrid."

"Very well," Dacre answered, "if that is your decision, you have only yourself to blame, Miss Somerton. See you in Weymouth—if you still take an interest in journalism."

He knew they were behaving like two schoolchildren, that he was acting ungallantly, that he ought to have been tarred and feathered, but he decided this girl should have a lesson, and he started the car forward. His rate of progress was deliberately slow, for he was curious to see if she would relent, so he watched her carefully for a few minutes, but Lena was striding back on the return journey to the hotel.

It all seemed ghastly absurd, yet it was a challenge of sub-temperaments, and the battle would have to be fought out one time or another.

But there came a dramatic interruption.

It was the sudden appearance of an airplane.

Like a bolt from the blue, it darted out of the sky, sank to a distance of four thousand feet, and then commenced circling round. The drone of the engines was strange and sinister-like.

Dacre gasped.

Lena ran back to him.

That circling motion! It recalled to both of them what Gutteridge reported yesterday! Was it only coincidence, or good heavens, did it mean that—?

"Look!" Lena exclaimed. "That plane behaves exactly like the one yesterday, and it's right over Cottingdale! What does it mean, Dacre? What's going on up there? No need to circle about in that fashion. What the mischief is he playing at?"

They were both pilots, and they had a technical knowledge of machines. Dacre got out of his car, and moved over to the nearest gate. The girl joined him in a strange silence, and they both stared at the gyratory motion of the machine.

Dacre held his breath.

Automatically he pushed the gate open.

He did not know what was coming, or what was going to happen, but he had a terrible presentiment that something was wrong. There was something damned funny about that airplane. It soared round and round!

Five times—seven—nine.

The awful spin went on.

Dacre counted, just like Gutteridge the previous day . . . Twelve. Fourteen. Seventeen times in one circle!

Then, good God—!

Horror of horrors!

Lena clutched at his arm. Her eyes closed for an instant, then stared upward.

Dacre never moved.

He saw that awful thing happen. Saw that human body hurtle from the machine to the earth—two hands hurled it from the cockpit—and down, down it came into space. Then the plane dashed back into the heavens.

But this time there was no hayrick.

Lena shivered, and hid her face.

The body crashed into a neighbouring field—the one slightly to their left—and then there followed a horrible silence.

"My God, did you see that?" the expert asked in a steely voice.

Lena swayed against him. She was sick and dizzy with the awful spectacle. There in the bright sunlight, in the face of Heaven itself, another ghoulish tragedy had been committed before their eyes.

So Gutteridge had been right after all.

Cambon and others had mocked—!

But there was a vampire of some kind in the sky! A human fiend. A madman of some sort.

Lena came to her senses first. Her nerves were unstrung, her lovely face blanched, but she saw the necessity for action.

Dacre was stunned.

Then he moved. He took to his heels and ran forward.

"Hurry—hurry!" Lena shouted after him, running as fast as she could. "Perhaps we may be in time! Perhaps—!" Oh, she did not know what to think. The tears ran down her cheeks.

They reached the spot in a few minutes, but a single glance was sufficient.

They stepped back appalled.

The body was crushed beyond all recognition. Yet some of the features were intact, and then Dacre pushed her back. He did not want her to see, but that terrible spectacle met her eyes, and she almost fainted.

The girl had been murdered before being flung from the machine, stabbed to death like Ruth Henderson, and just above the breast. Her clothes were torn at that spot, and the naked flesh was revealed. Dacre was down on his knees. He saw the marks of the same human teeth. The vampire had drunk the blood of this victim also!

CHAPTER VII

A PAIR OF SHOES

LENA FOUND she was a real woman.

The tears were streaming down her face.

She forgot all about journalism in that moment.

"Oh Dacre, this is more than I can stand," she moaned. "I have never seen anything like this in my life. Look, ever so many people are running across the fields. Here is someone in uniform. Surely that can't be the famous Gutteridge—!"

No, it was not Gutteridge. It was Inspector Frank Murray, his superior officer. He had seen the airplane sensation with his own eyes, and never stopped running until he reached the field.

He rushed across to Dacre and bent down.

"No mistake this time, sir," he gasped. "I am a Crown witness as well as yourself, and poor old Gutteridge is as sane as the rest of us. I saw the whole thing from the corner of the road. I saw the body fall from the plane, saw it being hurled from the cockpit just like a sack, and then I knew something terrible had happened. Oh God, isn't it awful. Look, the same ugly knife-wound above the breast, the same savage teeth drawing the blood—Ugh, the sight makes me sick!"

Dacre glanced up for a second.

He rather liked Murray.

He was a bigger humanitarian than most men.

"Inspector," he said, "oblige me by putting all these people out of the field. Tell them it is an order from me. You might also take a few names in case we want additional witnesses. I am going to see if this poor girl can be identified, and certainly we don't want a gaping crowd of farm labourers."

"Very good, sir!" The Inspector was glad to move away for a few seconds. The sight of that murdered body was almost unnerving. He lifted his hand with a Governmental air of authority, and asked everyone to transfer themselves to the road. It was an awkward second. The farm labourers and countryfolk showed signs of rebellion, for a sensation like this was not provided every Sunday morning, and they had known nothing like it in all Cottingdale history. But when a burly constable appeared he brought additional weight, and the significant move he made to his truncheon was alarming. Yes, it would be better to pay some respect to the law, so they allowed themselves to be pushed back as far as the gate, but at that strategic position they stuck and remained.

Dacre went on with his investigation. He made a critical survey of the knife-wound, carefully examined the throat and neck, and then scanned the features dispassionately.

He noticed this girl was more respectably dressed. She possessed an air of gentility that was absent in Ruth Henderson. Apparently she had come of a good-class family, and the face was decidedly pretty. Her age could not have been more than twenty-one.

But she wore no jewellery of any kind, and there were no letters of identification in her pocket. Doubtless she had left her small bag in the machine. The only clue was the pair of new shoes on her feet. They could not have been purchased more than twenty-four hours, and they bore the name and address of a Weymouth boot-house. Dacre jotted it down in his book:

MARCHLAND & CO.,
17 Upper Brook Street,
WEYMOUTH.

Then he turned to look for Lena Somerton, and saw she had vanished. Had the spectacle of murder been too much for her, and had she allowed Murray to put her out of the field?

He was a trifle surprised at the incident. Then he jumped at the solution. She had probably dashed off to the nearest telephone.

But then women were always treacherous!

She was more concerned with her newspaper "scoop," than the thought of assisting him in the crisis.

Bah, they were all the same.

He rose to his feet with a little sigh.

This second crime verified his thesis—he had submitted that already to Chief-Constable Muir—but it perturbed him nevertheless. He was horrified beyond words at the tragedy, but what lay behind it all, and why had the Cottingdale area been selected? Did it mean—?

Murray returned to him in a few seconds.

"Any clue?" he ventured.

Dacre shrugged his shoulders.

He pointed to the shoes, and the name and address they bore.

"Only one of possible identity," he said in an enigmatic voice. "But, Murray, I have got some special work for you, and I know you won't let me down. First of all, nothing can be gained by the body lying in this field. I want it removed at once to Cottingdale Police Station, and you had better notify Dr. Gibbs to examine it. I want to see if the same kind of knife was used. I feel certain in the matter, but it is better to have his confirmation."

Inspector Murray gave a sharp salute.

"Very good, Mr. Dacre," he answered, "I will have those instructions carried out immediately. Is there anything else?"

"Yes, you might phone through to all the air stations. Say nothing to them about the murder at present—thank God Fleet Street is quiet to-day—but find out what machine has passed over Cottingdale, ascertain if you can the direction, and get all the particulars they can give you. You might also speak to the Air Force Headquarters in London, give them the same message, and ask them to find out by wireless what we want. There must be no time lost, Inspector. Every moment now is of tremendous importance."

"Very good, Mr. Dacre, I will get busy at once," and Murray flew like a schoolboy training for the hundred yards!

Police-Constable Stevens moved forward. He felt almost as important as P.C. Gutteridge, and secretly he wondered if his own photograph would be in the papers. He had seen the airplane tragedy, or sensation, or whatever you like to call it. Hang it all, there was not a single camera-man about. Still, the reporters would be along in a jiffy. What a tale he would spin them!

Dacre drew him on one side.

"Look here, Stevens, you have got a simple job to do. Just see those people are kept outside that gate, and let none of them approach here on any consideration. Inspector Murray will arrange to have the body transferred to the Police Station, and you must remain on guard until that is done. I have an important call to make, but if I do not get back before Doctor Gibbs, tell him to examine that knife-wound carefully, and to let me have his official report before lunch. He will understand what I mean!"

The constable drew himself up.

He showed a spark of intelligence.

That was because he went in for the Pelman system.

"Very good, sir," he replied. "You suspect the same kind of knife was used in this case, and you want the verification in writing from Dr. Gibbs."

Dacre was almost stupefied. Never in his career had he encountered such a genius.

"My dear fellow, it's a brain-wave," he said enthusiastically. "However did you work it out !—Well, try and get a coat of some kind and put it over that body. As you can see, it is crushed almost beyond recognition, and we don't want those women-folk fainting along the road."

The constable moved off in search of a coat, which he borrowed temporarily from a farm labourer, and then Dacre gave a start of recognition.

A familiar figure had entered through the gate.

It was none other than Dr. Philip Gibbs.

He strode forward, huge, jovial, and important-looking as ever.

"Hillo, Dacre," he said breezily, "just met Inspector Murray coming along in my car. He gave me a rough outline of what has happened, and he tells me you are very anxious to see me . . . Good Lord . . . ."

His eyes went swiftly to the motionless form.

He was prepared for the shock, but it almost took his breath away.

A crime yesterday. A crime to-day! He was staggered.

"Yes, have a glance at that!" Dacre said dramatically. "It is almost a repetition of what occurred yesterday, Gibbs, and we have got to go through the same formalities. All of us here saw the tragedy with our own eyes, and I only beat Inspector Murray by a short head . . . That wound above the breast, doctor. I believe the same kind of knife has been used, and I want you to confirm that as soon as you can."

Gibbs was on his knees beside the murdered girl.

His professional gaze was fixed on that a terrible sight.

He stared critically at this second victim.

"Say, Dacre," he exclaimed in a hoarse voice, "this sort of thing is getting too popular. You will have to put a stop to this business, otherwise no one is going to enter a plane under a thousand pounds . . . Your suspicion is correct, my friend. Precisely the same kind of knife has been used, and the murderer has been up to the same tricks. God, look at the marks of those teeth. Well, I'm damned . . . Can you beat it, Constable, for downright horror?"

The policeman shook his head.

"Must be the work of a lunatic, sir," he replied.

"Haven't the faintest doubt about it," Gibbs muttered. "Why, I think it's even a reflection on insane people. No one but a wild animal could have done a thing like this. Dacre, I'm aghast—positively aghast. The sooner I get home for a drop of brandy the better!"

The Yard man nodded.

"It's almost too terrible for description," he agreed. "The machine circled over us about seventeen times, and when that business started I thought of Gutteridge yesterday. It jumped into my head that something was wrong, and when the thing happened, I was almost expecting it!"

"You couldn't make out the type of plane?"

"I thought at first it was a Gypsy Moth, then I saw it was much too big for that. All those planes are much alike, Gibbs, when they are four or five thousand feet up. I have proved it by experience. Yet I am certain of one thing. It did not seem to me like a Government plane. I may be wrong, of course, but that was the impression that flashed across my mind. And as regards the engine, it hummed like an eight-cylinder rotary."

The doctor took another glance at the dead girl's face.

He examined the crushed body, and once again shuddered.

"But I can't understand how the poor thing was duped," he protested. "Surely everyone saw the papers, Dacre! If that was not a clear warning to keep clear of airplanes, and suspicious strangers offering one a joyride—"

Dacre gave a grim smile.

"That is just the point," he replied. "You would be surprised at the number of people who do not glance at a paper, who never even dream of buying one. Besides, Gibbs, the man who coaxed that girl in his machine was no fool. He must be an individual with a very plausible personality, with the most charming manners in the world, and with an unlimited amount of money, otherwise that poor girl would never have been hoaxed."

Gibbs rose to his feet.

"You will have my official report before lunch," he observed. "I will send it along to the Police Station. I can do no more at the moment. That knife-thrust meant instant death, Dacre, and there is not the slightest doubt about what happened afterwards. The fiend drank her life-blood. It's the most ghoulish thing I have known in my career."

Dacre accompanied him as far as the gate.

Then his eyebrows lifted in surprise. There was no sign of the car. Nor of Lena either. Apparently both had vanished.

Well, she had a nerve to take the car. Surely she might have known that he had to get to Mountdale. Then he smiled. An idea entered his head. Perhaps she had stolen a march on him? Perhaps she had dashed off to reconnoitre?

He would wait.

He would see what happened.

She was bound to return with that car.

He turned suddenly to the medical doctor.

"Say, Gibbs, do you know a man in these parts named Major Frank Hardy?" The crowd had fallen back to their position at the gate. Gibbs had clambered into his waiting motorcar, and Dacre leaned against the side of it.

The doctor gave a curt nod.

He glanced at his watch. He had time for three more patients before lunch!

"Major Frank Hardy?" he echoed. "Why, of course I know the fellow. I am not to be regarded as his family practitioner, but I have paid him one or two visits. He suffers at intervals from an attack of asthma. Bit of a funny cove, you know, but then I suppose we are all on the border-line of madness. Why do you ask?"

Dacre glanced round. There was no one within earshot.

"I am making a few enquiries about him," he continued. "I understand he is wealthy, very independent, and possesses an airplane."

Gibbs grinned.

"He possesses everything except a wife," he retorted. "But there is no harm in him having an airplane, Dacre. Now if it was an airship you might talk, but great heavens, these planes are as common as blackberries. Why, in a few more years I will be careering about in a Gypsy Moth myself, perhaps paying my calls from the air at 3*s*. 6*d*. a time!"

He was trying to laugh, for the atmosphere of that field depressed him. The moment Dacre stopped asking idiotic questions, he would be away like a shot. Two murders in two days were sufficient for any doctor!

Then he turned and glared at the expert.

"Good Lord, Dacre, you don't imagine that—?"

"I never imagine anything," Dacre corrected. "That is a luxury I cannot afford. Like the French, I prefer realism, my dear Gibbs, and for that reason I want the truth about Hardy. Why does he use an airplane? Is it for business or pleasure, and how much can you tell me about him?"

Gibbs yawned.

He was feeling positively bored.

"Well, if you must know," he answered, "Hardy is a gentleman of leisure. He follows no particular profession. He can get up with the lark or go to bed with the milkman—if you will forgive me putting it that way. As regards his old skyrocket, I know he travels a good deal by air. He can drive as well as any British pilot, and I believe he thinks nothing of a flip to Berlin, or any other part of the world. It all depends on his mood. Goes away for six weeks at a time. That's the kind of life, my boy. One day I will aspire to it!"

Dacre stared at him hard.

"You referred just now to his eccentricity. In what way does he strike you as original, Gibbs?"

The doctor stroked his moustache.

He could understand now why some detectives were shot!

"Well," he said thoughtfully, "he is a chap with a very explosive temper, and when that happens, you may be certain of an earthquake. He sort of goes mad for a few minutes, and all kinds of things happen. I believe the servants are terrified of him in that state. He has been known to smash everything in the library, to break every pane of glass in the conservatory, and to threaten everyone with murder. I have warned him about his temper on several occasions, and one of these days he may go off in a flash. Heart, you know, is not too robust!"

Dacre expressed his thanks.

Gibbs went away exceedingly well pleased with himself.

The expert had stopped asking questions.

But there was a reason for that.

Away in the distance, driving her car like someone chased by ten thousand furies, was the fascinating figure of Lena Somerton, and she was coming straight in his direction.

She had been to Mountdale.

CHAPTER VIII

A CRASH

MALCOLM DACRE stood in the centre of the road.

The car rushed towards him at a breakneck speed.

He waited patiently.

"Well," he said, as Lena reached him and pulled up, "what sensational discovery did you make at Mountdale?"

The girl gave a little disjointed laugh.

The red beret made her a picture of loveliness.

Even Dacre was impressed with that fact.

"Look here, Big Boy," she said triumphantly, "I guess you want to put more pep into this detective business. While you were dithering about with a dead body in that field, I was getting real information first-hand. I have been to Mountdale as you say, and have found out something of importance."

Dacre leaned forward. He was gazing into her blue eyes. She was dazzlingly alluring at that instant.

"What is it?" he demanded.

"Major Frank Hardy is not in residence. Nor his airplane either. Both he and the machine have been absent two days from Mountdale, but he is expected back before lunch. He may return at any moment."

The expert looked thoughtful.

"Whom did you see?"

"I saw Mrs. Trelawney who keeps the porter-lodge. I gave her to understand I was a journalist, that I had come to interview Major Hardy for my paper, and that I should like to see him at once."

Dacre grinned.

This girl was something different to "Alice in Wonderland"!

Even a gangster could find nothing on her!

"What else?"

"She is rather a decent kind of woman," Lena continued, "and soon we were chatting like old friends. But she was strangely reticent about Major Hardy. All she would admit was that he was peculiar, and she gave me a warning about his terrific temper. She said if the Major happened to be in a bad mood to leave Mountdale at once. When he goes into one of his Oriental tantrums, he is not responsible for his actions. Beyond that she would not commit herself."

Dacre tried to look stern.

He found it a difficult process.

The blue eyes were melting and mildly provoking.

"Why did you bolt off in that fashion?" he queried. "For all you know, you may have upset the whole applecart. Nothing is worse to me than a bad blunder. There is no reason in the world to suspect Hardy, or anyone round these parts, but even supposing I had some data, your appearance as a newspaper woman might give the show away. You see, I intended my visit to be a most casual one. Anything deliberate would spoil my plans."

Lena flashed him a look of scorn.

It was a glance of cool, unmitigated contempt.

Yet the carmine flush remained on her cheeks.

"I have already said you were a mug," she replied disdainfully. "Don't you realise what I tried to do, and don't you think I deserve a medal? This man Hardy has aroused your curiosity, and you were anxious for a report about him. Had he been the potential murderer, you would have wanted to know something about his plane, and what he was doing at present. I have found out that he and his machine are missing. Both are absent from Mountdale. So where have they been in the interim? Mrs. Trelawney has not the faintest possible idea, so I leave you to figure it out!"

Dacre realised she deserved commendation.

Yet he was loath to bestow praise on a girl.

She had merely tried to score over him!

"All the same, I prefer to conduct this case in my own way," he ventured. "Inspiration on your part is one thing, Miss Somerton, but to me it may only represent foolishness, which means I should like to do my own brainwork."

Lena jumped out of the car and frowned.

Dacre seemed the most objectionable creature alive!

Frankly she hated him.

"Don't be too sure I was working on your behalf," she retorted. "As a matter of truth, I went to Mountdale as a representative of the *Sentinel*. We are dealing now with two murder mysteries, Mr. Dacre, and I am as much preoccupied with airplanes as you are. If you have any objection to what I have done, you have my permission to go and commit suicide."

"You can't do as you please with that car," he protested.

"The car does not belong to you," she said wickedly. "It was merely loaned to you by the Chief Constable, and if he had seen me he would have made me a free gift of it. But there, it is plain we cannot co-operate. I am going back to the hotel to write my report, and to get through to Fleet Street as soon as possible."

Dacre held up his hand.

They were acting like children in the middle of a stupendous crisis.

How ridiculous it all seemed!

"One moment," he begged. "As you have rendered me a service, perhaps you had better hear the latest news. The Press Association men will be here in a few seconds, so I want you to consider yourself privileged. You may say that I hope to establish identity, and that although the body is almost unrecognisable, I believe I have secured one definite pointer. That will keep them guessing, and prove to the editor you have not been asleep."

Lena's lip curled.

She had all the instincts of a journalist.

Plainly her curiosity was aroused.

"Listen, Sherlock Holmes," she announced, "any schoolboy reporter could write that stuff. I have a distinct craving for news, and nothing but news with a capital N will satisfy my sub-editorial Chief. If you are speaking now only about identity, there is no need to be reticent like an archbishop. Spin out the details and leave the rest to the Almighty!"

But Dacre was adamant for once.

"Better let it go at that," he temporised. "I want to make discreet enquiries in this case, and there are occasions in life when a newspaper may be a confounded nuisance. This is one of them."

Lena moved a step nearer.

Was it possible that Dacre was not the fool he looked?

She was afflicted with a desire to help him.

"Look here," she added, "there is something I almost forgot. You happen to be a stranger in these parts, and all you have got is a tourist map. So much for your intelligence, but for your information, Mountdale is on the other side of those hills. In fact, to be perfectly accurate, you will find it on the other side of that mountain. The road sweeps round in a circular curve about a mile distant. My friend, if you had an air ticket at Northolt you know what that means."

Dacre gave an appreciative nod.

This girl was more intelligent than she appeared.

She really possessed grey matter.

"You wish me to understand," he said swiftly, "that Major Frank Hardy could land from the other side, that his descent would be screened from this point of vantage?"

"Precisely. Now think the rest out for yourself, for I am going to get through to Fleet Street. Thank heaven, this is Sunday, and there is no edition until to-morrow morning. Where shall I find you?"

Dacre jumped into the car.

"I am going back to the hotel to ring up the Yard," he said quietly. "If you promise to behave yourself, you can come along with me that distance." He broke off suddenly, for a policeman came dashing along on a motor cycle, and pulled up in a flash when he reached the Yard expert. Dismounting, he gave a swift salute and his message.

"I have been sent along from the Chief Constable, sir!" he said breathlessly. "An airplane has crashed on the other side of Mountdale, and the news has just come through by telephone. The Chief thought you might like to investigate, and as I had the field described to me, I can take you there in about five minutes."

Dacre started his car and Lena jumped in beside him.

"Lead the way!" he ordered.

The constable started off at a good pace, and the police car kept close behind. The crash might only mean a side-issue, but every plane in the vicinity had to be carefully watched. As the car flew along, Dacre wondered if he was going to be favoured by the gods? Was it possible the vampire of the skies had met his doom? Did it mean that a Higher judge had taken the matter into His Supreme Court?

Lena seemed to read his thoughts.

Her features changed colour for an instant.

She was stimulated by the thrill of it all.

"Is it the man we both want," she speculated, "or has Major Hardy met with this accident on his return journey?"

"We will see in a few seconds," Dacre answered. "One thing is evident. No other plane passed over this part except the one we saw—or if it did it was at a tremendous altitude—but if you say Mountdale is on the other side of that hill, I conceive the possibility of a machine getting down behind it. In that case it may mean that the gallant Major has crashed."

They turned the bend of the road at last, and soon they were racing in the direction of the three hills. Lena explained that Mountdale was more on the right, but the constable was taking the road that led to the left. That was significant. It was the most exciting drive Lena ever experienced. She fancied herself able to move at the wheel, but Dacre beat all records in that respect. He was a perfect demon of speed.

Then at last they saw the wrecked airplane. It lay overturned in one of the fields far distant, and Dacre saw with a feeling of relief it had not caught fire. He wanted, at all cost, to examine the interior of that machine, no matter what excuse the pilot offered about the crash. If there were signs of blood—!

When the field was reached, Dacre pulled up the car and sprang out. Lena followed at his heels. The constable was already opening the gates. A small crowd of people gazed at them curiously.

Then out of the group a man detached himself.

It was the pilot, and he recognised Dacre in a flash.

"Just the man I want to see," he exclaimed, seizing the expert by the hand and wringing it fervently. "My name is Holmes, Mr. Dacre—Captain Trevor Holmes—and I belong to the Air Force. You phoned through to the Ministry last night, and I got my flying orders this morning. I was told to reconnoitre this locality, to make a detailed report concerning any aircraft, and then to get in touch with you afterwards. This is the way I've done it. Don't I deserve the Air Medal?"

Before uttering a word, Dacre observed it was a Government machine, and a glance at the pilot showed he was shaken but not hurt. Apparently he had crawled from the plane without mishap. It had been a close shave.

"I am glad you got out of this alive," Dacre muttered. "You are perfectly sure, Holmes, you are not injured? No bones broken, I trust?"

Captain Trevor Holmes was more than passably good looking. He had a tall, upright figure, and his air uniform revealed it to perfect advantage. He had grey eyes that constantly twinkled, a perfectly ridiculous moustache, and a mouth that spoke of courage. There was something prepossessing about his youthful boyish face, and Lena Somerton had an absurd idea she would like to kiss it. At any rate, he might be eligible for a possible flirtation.

"I'm absolutely O.K.," Holmes answered. "But these country folk think it is a miracle. When the plane crashed, they expected the usual developments—the engine going on fire and the charred remains of a poor pilot. I object to being burnt alive. Nothing would put me in a worse temper."

He stared rather forcibly at Lena as he spoke, gave her a swift salute, and then waited for an introduction. Dacre complied with the formalities.

"But what on earth happened?" Lena demanded at once. "Here is a perfect field for a landing, Captain Holmes, and you think it eminently suitable for a somersault. You know, Government planes are really expensive. I suppose that fact has percolated through your subconscious brain?"

Holmes burst into an uproarious laugh.

This was a girl after his own heart.

Heaven be praised, but his calamity had proved fortuitous after all.

"I only wish I could smash three or four a day," he replied with perfect good humour. "Unfortunately this happens to be my first crash, and I am none too proud of it. It is a perfect field, as you remark, Miss Somerton, but if you want to know the truth, I was rather late in shutting off the engine, and you know what that means. I came down a little faster than I anticipated, and it took me all my time to avert a nose-dive. In that case I would have been in the soup."

They strolled across and examined the wrecked machine.

Dacre saw the damage with a critical eye.

Both wings were smashed, and the engine looked in imminent danger of falling out.

Then he turned to the constable.

"Get back and explain matters to the Chief," he ordered. "Tell him to send the necessary message through to the Air Ministry, and inform him that I have completed my investigation. He will understand if you tell him!"

The constable gave a sharp salute and went off.

Dacre stared after the motor cycle for a few seconds, then he spoke again to the pilot.

"Well," he asked, "what was the result of your reconnaissance, Holmes?"

That individual shrugged his shoulders in disgust.

"My dear chap," he replied, "I have just come here direct from Farnborough aerodrome, and all I met on the journey was a tremendous flock of sea-gulls."

"Sea-gulls!" Dacre muttered. "Then you were gazing in the wrong direction. Would you be surprised to know that there has been another airplane tragedy?"

Holmes swung round with an oath.

"Not another murder, Mr. Dacre?" he protested.

The expert nodded.

"Almost a repetition of what occurred yesterday," he continued. Briefly he recounted what happened, and Holmes listened with almost incredulous dismay. Then he glanced back at his damaged plane.

"By God," he groaned, "if I had only not made that false landing. Look here, Dacre, let us for heaven's sake get in touch with the nearest telephone. Someone must have an airplane round these parts. If I can borrow it, I am prepared to spend all day searching for that devil with a knife. By all the saints, he must be mad—stark, staring mad!"

As if in answer to his impassioned outburst, Lena pointed suddenly up to the sky. Thousands of feet high, but coming from the direction of the Channel, was the faint speck of an airplane.

"It is Major Hardy!" she said instinctively. "He promised to get back to Mountdale before lunch. I feel certain that is his machine. There is your chance, Holmes, and if you don't take it, I will."

The pilot stared at her in bewilderment.

Dacre gave a quiet snigger.

Yet he was faintly thrilled.

"Miss Somerton is something more than a journalist," he explained. "She happens to have a pilot's certificate like yourself, Holmes, and I might add that I am in the same category. She is referring to a Major Hardy who lives at Mountdale. He has a machine of his own, but he has been absent two days, and that may be his plane returning. It is certainly heading this way. By Jove, I believe she is right. Look, he is wheeling round more in this direction. Mountdale is on the other side. He will shut the engine off soon."

They stared with all their might.

Lena felt in a mad whirl of excitement.

Was it the mysterious Hardy at last?

Then Holmes gave another solemn curse. He had no idea who Major Hardy might be, but he realised what was happening up aloft. That chap in the plane overhead had no more idea of coming down than the man in the moon. Almost before they could realise what his intentions were, the mystery man in the plane shot away above the clouds, and in a few seconds he was absolutely lost to view.

Lena Somerton wished that Holmes would curse afresh.

He did!

CHAPTER IX

HOLMES FALLS IN LOVE!

"I DO WISH you would teach me a few of those swear words!" Lena exclaimed. "Mr. Dacre is too conventional for worlds, but I think he swore that time. You see, Holmes, we may as well let you share a state secret. Major Frank Hardy happens to be a first-class mystery. He is a super-creature of unlimited wealth, owns that wonderful mansion over there on the left, and possesses a private plane. He takes a flip to Paris or Berlin when the mood seizes him, and for two days has failed to give an account of himself. His machine cannot be found, and I think our Yard friend would like to ask him a few questions!"

The Air Force pilot made a grimace.

It was a sign that he comprehended.

He was intrigued with the girl's beret.

"So that is how the wind blows," he muttered. "Well, let us hope Dacre has cottoned on to something. I expect he will be busy during the next few days, and in that case I may see more of you. I shall pray that they give me forty-eight hours' leave from Headquarters—they may grant me a full ten days—and in that case I might be able to help. Where are you staying at present?"

Dacre had wandered over to the wrecked airplane.

He never left anything to chance.

He wanted to make a more thorough inspection.

"I have stayed overnight at the 'White Hart' hotel," Lena replied with a shrug. "That is right in the centre of Cottingdale, and we will drive you there in a few minutes. I know you will join us at lunch. This afternoon I may leave for Weymouth. You see, I am on the staff of the London *Senti-*

nel, and I am desperately involved in these crimes. I wish to make a few discreet enquiries in Weymouth, and if I pick up anything important, I have promised to pass it on to Dacre. He and I are working in collaboration. He supplies the Scotland Yard energy, and I the brains!"

She laughed nervously at her own joke.

Holmes thought her ever so ravishing.

He had fallen in love at first sight.

"Great Cincinnati," he exclaimed, "I shall be delighted to lunch with you at that hotel. I am simply charmed we have met, Miss Somerton. You know, I have been looking for a girl like you for ages. A girl with a red beret, a divine figure, and two audacious blue eyes. Try and forgive me paying you such a terrific compliment, but I really cannot help myself."

Lena gave him the "once over."

Yes, he was handsome, but she saw complications.

A complex situation amused her vastly.

"Never mind the compliments," she said gravely. "As I told you just now, I am more interested in these ghastly crimes. I saw something this morning I shall never forget. I saw a murdered girl's body in that Cottingdale field, and I don't think I am going to sleep for a fortnight. Yes, it brought the tears I assure you. I cried almost like a baby . . . By the way, honeysuckle, if you are going to get official leave, there is a chance I may find work for you. Say nothing more for the present. I only get an idea once a year!"

"Word of honour!" Holmes whispered.

He would have loved to kiss her.

Never had he seen anyone so enchanting.

She was stupendously lovely!

"Let's get back to the hotel," Dacre suggested, returning to their side. "A horde of reporters will descend on us immediately, and we had better give them the slip."

"Not this one," Lena said maliciously.

"Worse luck," Dacre muttered.

He saw that Holmes was already ensnared by the girl-journalist, and that made him more irritable than ever. Why the furies did girls intrude upon men? Why could they not live their own lives, keep their own sphere, and grow canaries in the back kitchen?

"Dacre, I want your advice," Holmes said promptly. "Miss Somerton has not yet promised to marry me, but she has invited me to lunch at the 'White Hart' Hotel. Fancy being asked to lunch by so charming a personage! May I consider it a bona fide invitation? She tells me you are acting as her fairy godfather."

The expert restrained a smile.

Lena was hiding her face.

It was aflame with colour.

"My dear chap, you are more than welcome," he responded. "Come along by all means and forget your troubles. I assure you the food is excellent, the wine is beyond criticism, and you can stay as long as you like!"

"Providing you pay your bill," Lena said whimsically.

They entered the car with Dacre at the wheel, and soon it was flying down the long stretch of road. Holmes and Lena occupied the back seat, and the young pilot kept her amused with the very latest air stories. In repayment, Lena confided to him one or two Fleet Street "ghost" stories that made him roar!

But Dacre was paying little attention to them. He was preoccupied with the second crime, and the horror of it still haunted him. It showed him he must act with promptitude. The "Vampire" was more mentally alert than he imagined. Why, there might even be a third or fourth crime! Heaven forbid such further tragedy, but everything pointed to it. That was providing Dacre could not get on the track. At all costs that madman of the skies must be outwitted. If necessary, the entire Air Force would be requisitioned to hunt down that ghoulish murderer.

Once or twice his thoughts strayed to Cambon. Should he ring up his French colleague and consult him? He might like to hear of this second outrage. Certainly his cynical comments would be amusing, but would anything be gained by a phone chat? Cambon was a stupendous paradox! Perhaps he should be ignored for the present.

Dacre stopped the car when he reached Cottingdale Police Station.

He turned to the pair behind him.

Holmes was sitting suspiciously close.

And what was his right arm doing?

"I am going to have a word with the Chief Constable," Dacre announced. "Under those circumstances, Miss Somerton, may I beg of you to see that Captain Holmes is not starved? If you drive him to the 'White Hart' Hotel, I will try and get along soon. You can order lunch for three famished people, but do not wait for me if I am detained."

"I should never dream of that," Lena responded pertly, taking her place at the wheel. "Captain Holmes is divine! He has kept me enthralled with the most amazing stories, and I am telling him all the naughtiest in my brainbox. Say Dacre, you really will remember lunch, won't you? After all, grey matter cannot flourish on a fasting stomach, and you are looking as if a cocktail might inspire you to fresh energy. Do hurry, please, and I will get through to Fleet Street in the interim."

She gave the expert a cheery wave of the hand, and then burst out laughing when she noticed he was bombarded by three London reporters. She knew them all, and thanked heaven she was first on the London line.

As for Dacre, he tried to think of the last swear word used by Holmes. That was impossible, so, squaring his shoulders, he allowed himself to be sucked dry like an orange. He gave all the dramatic details, watched them gasp with horror and amazement, and then pushed them gently away. They were delightful boys but a confounded nuisance!

When he strolled into the station, he was confronted by the dignified figure of P.C. Gutteridge.

"Well, Mr. Dacre," he said breezily, "I hear our sky-friend missed the hayrick this time. Gosh, if we only had one of those anti-aircraft guns! But wait. Perhaps next time he's round this district we will have a special way of bringing him down."

"Wish you could think of something," Dacre grinned with perfect good humour. "But it proves you were not intoxicated yesterday, Gutteridge, or suffering from an evil imagination either. They all tried to poke fun at you, that bally Frenchman included, but you stood up boldly for the truth. One day you will be an angel, and then how Monsieur Cambon will laugh! . . . Our flying devil went through the same programme to-day. Circled round us about seventeen times—I wonder what magic is in that number—then dropped his terrible burden to the earth. I assure you, Gutteridge, it was something I shall never forget. Lunch is the last thing I could touch at present. I could even do with a sip of your brandy. But where is the Chief? I want to see him at once."

"I believe he is expecting you to call, sir," Gutteridge said promptly, proud to be on such familiar terms with the Scotland Yard ace. "You will find him right in his private office—and if you want that nip of brandy, Mr. Dacre—?"

The expert shrugged, then moved along the passage.

"No, not at present, thanks," he replied. "My critics might think it a sign of weakness, forgetting for the moment I am perfectly human. But never sign the pledge, Gutteridge. It is absolutely bad form nowadays."

The constable pushed open the door of the Chief Constable's room, made his salute and announcement, then ushered the expert inside with a bow.

But Dacre did not sit down.

"Hullo, Chief," he said cordially, "I want to thank you for rushing through that message about the crashed plane. If you have no objection, I am going to use your London phone. I must speak to the Yard immediately!"

Chief Constable Muir sprang to his feet. "Go straight ahead, Mr. Dacre," he exclaimed. "You will find the London phone in the second room to the left, and I will see that no one disturbs you. I have just been waiting on a word with you. Am completely dumbfounded over this second crime. What a nerve that air-devil has got! It's the most sensational business in all my career! It means that Cottingdale is going down to history, but I wish some other dumping-ground had been selected."

Dacre gave a curt nod.

"It means also that I am a Crown witness," he declared. "I saw the ghastly sight with my own eyes, Chief, and I never want to have the same experience. Your Inspector Murray rendered us very important help, and I want you to see that it is recognised. I presume the body has been brought to the Station? Those were my instructions."

"We have it in a special room," Muir responded. "It can remain here until after the inquest, but honestly, Mr. Dacre, I could hardly bear to look at the horrible mutilation of flesh. It sickened me at once. Never in the whole course of my official career—"

"Well, I shall be back in a jiffy," Dacre interrupted, and dashed off to the London phone.

Inside an incredibly short time he got through to the Yard, and three seconds later was speaking to his own Chief. As he quite anticipated, Sir Francis Didgett was appalled by the terrible tidings. Breathlessly he listened while Dacre recounted the details, also the news about the plane crash, but Didgett did not appear concerned over that incident.

"Blast Holmes," he said irritably. "Pity the fool did not break his neck. Fancy acting the silly ass stunt when we badly wanted his help. So long as he is clear of any suspicion, he can well take care of himself. But, Dacre, I want to be perfectly honest. This is serious news about a second airplane murder. Now why the devil was the Cottingdale area selected? What's the big idea? Well, you must move heaven and earth, my boy, to find the fiend, and give him no quarter if he slips into your hands. By heavens, there will be some newspaper talk over this. I can hear those Fleet Street machines buzzing already!"

"Never mind Fleet Street," Dacre counselled. "Our plan is to sit tight and say nothing. But as you say, Chief, we have got to move heaven and earth. What I beg you to do is this: use every ounce of influence at your command, and get the Air Force heads to make the most drastic enquiries. Let them send as many air scouts out as possible, but not to complicate my own plans. Holmes, of course, had nothing to do with this business, but every plane in the Cottingdale area will be suspect until I find my man. You understand?"

"Quite, I will attend to that point," the Chief promised.

"Those special Air reports reached me this morning," Dacre continued, "but they contain next to nothing. When all is said and done, Chief, our connecting links in the air world are not ultra-efficient. We want a tighter hold on these Government machines, and it is up to Whitehall to stop muddling the pilots. As regards the private planes owned by citizens, that is vastly more important. Can you let me have a list immediately?"

The Chief groaned.

"My God," he said, "you have asked me something. Why, that list will take days, Dacre, but you will have the Cottingdale group as fast as I can get hold of it. We are working like death up here on your behalf. The Air Force people have been at it all night, and a special staff has been engaged. No word of a pointer yet?"

Dacre thought of the bangle, but on that point he was silent.

"Nothing beyond a pair of shoes," he said sorrowfully. "They were sold to the second victim by a Weymouth bootshop, and we have got the name and address. It may lead to identity first thing in the morning. We want that established as soon as we can. But, Chief, there is another point I must stress, and for God's sake, see that it is not overlooked. Every police station in England must put up a warning notice. Until this air lunatic is caught, no girl will be safe to accept an airplane joy-ride from any stranger. I have a special reason for stressing that."

The Chief whistled.

"Good heavens," he exclaimed, "you don't mean—?"

"We are dealing with a human vampire," Dacre replied. "That implies, Chief, he will go on killing until he is hounded down. Remember, he has tasted the blood of two victims. He will go on slaking his awful thirst until we lay him cold."

"My God—!"

"Make no mistake about it, Chief. That is his programme. Now look here, I want a special Government plane. I have no time to mess about the preliminaries, so will you please get in touch with Whitehall, and have a plane sent down here by a special pilot. Let him fly direct to Cottingdale and land in the nearest field to the Police Station."

"I will send one down inside an hour, Dacre!"

"Splendid. Well now, for your own private ear, I have run across M. Cambon of the French *Sûreté*. I met him at Weymouth yesterday, where he is supposed to be staying on holiday, but, for all we know, he may have something up his sleeve about an English suspect. At any rate, he accompanied me down to Cottingdale, investigated the first crime, and then went back last night to Weymouth. He seems stupendously interested in this vampire business, and he wants me to give him a call. He is staying at Claridge's Hotel, Weymouth, but I am not impressed by his remarks. Cambon bores me to a certain extent."

Didgett groaned afresh.

"Good lord," he said irritably, "we don't want those French men worrying us at present. I have a righteous respect for every member of the Paris *Sûreté*, Dacre, but hang it all, I am not going to worship at that altar. Frankly, I have never cared much for Cambon, and if the latest rumour is correct, I hear he is on the point of retirement. He is clever, of course, but I believe he never scored popularity. Too confident about his own ideas, I think!"

Dacre sent a laugh over the wire.

"He is certainly original at times," he grinned, "and I confess I found him amusing. But one cannot afford to offend the *Sûreté*, Chief, so I have done my utmost to be *diplomatique*."

"Good. Well, never mind Cambon either. Tell me something about Major Frank Hardy. I sent you a special line about him. Any result? Have you tumbled across him yet?"

Dacre sighed.

"He is worse than the Scarlet Pimpernel," he replied. "He has been two days away from Mountdale, Chief, and his plane is missing as well. Rather an enigmatic gentleman, I believe, so a little chat won't do us any harm. He may be a perfectly honest diamond, but one never knows, does one?"

"One does not. At any rate, Dacre, we cannot afford any mysteries in the Cottingdale area, so I am relying on you to put Hardy in his right category. We seem to have little data about him at Headquarters, but doubtless that is because he is more of a Continental figure. Just track down his movements like a good chap!"

"Very good, Chief. I am told he is due back very soon—perhaps within the next couple of hours—so I will pump him for all I'm worth. My own impression, of course, is that the man we want is much further afield, but if he has the nerve to live right under our nose, then that nerve is going to be shattered."

He rang off in a few seconds and returned to Muir.

The Chief Constable awaited him in his private room.

He seemed a mass of anxiety.

"Well, Mr. Dacre," he enquired, "what about this young Air Force merchant? No bones broken, I hear!"

"Fate seems to be on his side," the expert responded. "He had the good fortune not to set fire to his engine—possibly the engine acted with more discretion than he did—and after the crash he crawled from the plane. Both wings and under-carriage were smashed, and the engine seems in a precarious condition. But Holmes is perfectly all right. He has gone back to the 'White Hart' with a young lady journalist from the London *Sentinel*, and I have promised to join them at lunch!"

The Chief Constable grinned.

"Is she—very pretty?"

"She is much better than that!" Dacre beamed. "I believe she would win first prize at any beauty competition. Her name is Lena Somerton, but good Lord, she is a handful! Simply impossible to shake her off. She wants a special story for the *Sentinel*, and she is determined to get every line of it. Can you suggest any new kind of poison? Something that would leave no trace?"

"I know the type," Muir laughed. "In my young days, Mr. Dacre, I found no cure for that disease. They are all incurable, and the bigger the beauty prize the more dangerous!"

"Well, Holmes is smitten badly already. But for your information, Muir, that young lady can manage a plane. I am having a Government machine sent down here at once, and as I have obtained my own ticket at Northolt, my flying knowledge may prove useful in the immediate future."

The Chief gasped.

"Well, that is news," he exclaimed. "Never knew you obtained the wings, Mr. Dacre. And you tell me the young lady can manage the joy-stick also? Well, miracles are on the increase. My old grandmother would turn in her grave!"

"We won't put her down as an Amy Johnson," Dacre warned, "but she might score in an emergency. I have thought of a plan. She will try to act as decoy for our vampire friend, and she will operate in Weymouth. Afterwards she will write an article about her adventures. You can drop a hint to the Weymouth police. Tell them not to interfere with that arrangement."

The Chief made a careful note.

"So long as you keep these young sirens employed," he argued, "there is a bigger chance for us to escape."

"I hate the sex like poison, Chief, but we have to live with them. Miss Somerton is going to interview P.C. Gutteridge, so better prepare him in advance. Tell him to take an extra shave, and for heaven's sake to mind his aspirates. At all costs, he must not contradict her."

The Chief laughed heartily.

Then he leaned forward.

"Now, Mr. Dacre, let us sober up," he begged. "Do tell me what you think of this awful business! Can you imagine anything more terrible than these crimes? I simply dread to look at the papers to-morrow. Poor old Cottingdale—one of the quietest hamlets in the United Kingdom—will be the cesspool of talk in twenty-four hours!"

Dacre shrugged.

"I am indifferent to newspapers," he remarked. "Personally I am more concerned about the identity of the second victim. Nothing can be done until the Weymouth shops open to-morrow. I expect the camera men will be here soon, and they will take the usual snaps. That is where the papers are appreciated by the Yard. I mean, when it comes to photographs, Fleet Street is unique. Little do those men dream of the endless work they save."

Then came a dramatic interruption.

A girl's voice raised in high excitement.

Then the stern reply of P.C. Gutteridge.

"You simply can't see him, young lady! He is engaged with the Chief, and my orders are—"

But Lena Somerton burst into the room.

"Come quick, Dacre!" she said breathlessly. "Another crash, and this time the plane is on fire! . . . I saw it from the hotel window, and Holmes and I dashed here in that car. It's over in the direction of Mountdale—and the pilot has landed safely by parachute!"

CHAPTER X

A SURPRISE FOR HARDY!

MAJOR FRANK HARDY gave a short laugh.

The parachute lay at his feet.

It seemed to amuse him vastly.

"I am not exactly a kangaroo," he remarked to Dacre, "but there was nothing to do but jump for it. Had I waited longer I should have been an angel! I saw the machine go into a nose-dive. I realised I had lost control, and that Death stared me in the face. I am not ready for Death, so I jumped into space!"

The airplane was burning in the next field.

The flames roared like a furnace.

No one could approach within fifty yards.

"Yes, but what happened before the nose-dive?" Dacre enquired. "Seems to me you must have made a false move. Did you shut the engine off too soon or too late? Or, before you shut off, did you turn the nose too far down? I have frequently made that mistake, but I have always regained control."

He was staring at Hardy closely.

So this was the owner of Mountdale! This was the mystery man he had to watch. Yes, he certainly looked a peculiar prize packet. There was something strange about that tall, angular body, something devilish odd about those deep, magnetic eyes. They appeared to be a bluish grey, and they never wavered in their penetrating stare. He was dressed in a suit of brown plus fours—rather a funny garb for an airplane—and his furry cloth cap made him look ridiculous.

Lena Somerton watched him under her red beret.

She stood a little apart with Holmes.

Both were fascinated by the burning plane.

"If you want the truth," Hardy replied, "I was upset by that other wrecked plane. It seemed like an evil omen, and I caught sight of it just as I was preparing to land. When I saw it so close to Mountdale, I think it gave me cold feet. I do not suggest it affected my nerve, but somehow it got upon my imagination. I suppose it preoccupied my mind."

Countryfolk approached from all sides.

But they had eyes for nothing but the burning plane.

One or two stared at Hardy curiously.

"Well, I am sorry you have lost your machine," Dacre continued. "I see it was a De Havilland Puss Moth, but there is not much of it to write home about. What a pity! I was hoping, Major Hardy, to borrow that plane. It might have been of tremendous service!"

"Borrow my plane!" Hardy echoed.

A curious glint entered the bluish grey eyes. The face scowled ominously. He was asking himself questions. Who the devil was this fellow, and what did he mean by his confounded insolence? Borrow his plane! The blood mounted to his forehead, his upper lip quivered, his whole body shook. Unmistakable signs that Hardy had an ungovernable temper. That report about him was correct.

Perhaps he was really insane!

He certainly did not look normal.

More like a mental case out on probation!

"I am afraid I have not introduced myself," proceeded the expert. "My name is Malcolm Dacre, and I belong to Scotland Yard. As you have been away for two days, I presume you did not hear about the airplane crime. I have been sent down on a mission of investigation, and as I have qualified as an air-pilot, I was going to ask the loan of your machine. You see, the murder was committed in an airplane, and I regret a second one occurred this morning. My job is to hunt down the murderer."

A transformation went over Hardy's face.

He became suddenly pale.

His lips twitched ominously.

"My dear chap," he said, "you must come along to Mountdale and tell me all about it. But not now, I beg of you. I am a trifle upset by that accident. You see, I have been away in Paris, and have only returned this moment. Since I left I have not seen a French or English paper, so I am quite at a disadvantage."

Dacre glanced across at the burning plane.

What secret did it contain?

Was that engine set on fire deliberately?

"Well," he replied, "that's kind of you to invite me to Mountdale. May I introduce my friends?"

"Why, of course!"

Dacre called the others forward, and soon all four were chatting with great freedom. Being a British air-pilot, Holmes never stood on ceremony with anyone, and although Lena had warned him about Hardy, he was in the mood for leg-pulling.

"Say, Hardy," he exclaimed, "you have not come down at all. You are really one up. You see, I did my best to set fire to my old bus, not having to pay the insurance money, but somehow the trick did not work. You have succeeded splendidly! And if my beastly bus had caught fire, then sure as Fate the parachute would not have opened. I never get any real luck!"

They were walking in the direction of the car.

The crowd still clustered near the plane.

A constable had arrived and was showing authority.

"I don't know what you tried to do, Holmes," responded the owner of Mountdale, "but I'm jolly certain you nearly caused my death. The sight of your wrecked plane gave me the cold shivers, especially as I intended coming down at this spot. Strange how a coincidence like that will alter everything."

"Remarkably strange!" Lena remarked in an odd voice.

The impish mood had deserted her.

There was something about Hardy she disliked.

His way of looking at her was loathsome.

"What crowd were you with in the War?" Holmes asked. He realised the Major had army service.

"Oh, the Devons, and I have been flying two years. I find a machine very convenient. There is no greater fun than a flight across the Channel, and you know that as well as I do. My De Havilland was a top-notcher, and I am sorry she has gone. I would like to give her a proper burial, for I was getting fond of that old engine. Still, I must get another machine in a few days. I am a busy man, Holmes, and I could never exist without a plane."

"Perhaps you are spiritually inclined?" Lena observed cynically. "Some people love to soar near Heaven, but personally I prefer *terra firma* and Fleet Street!"

"Don't be absurd," Dacre protested. "Every woman is an angel without wings—according to Bernard Shaw."

Holmes passed his cigarette case.

"I could never stick a De Havilland," he replied. "It always made me say my prayers, and I hate to be a hypocrite. If I had any choice, my selection would be a Bristol Fighter. A trifle heavy, I admit, but they turn out wonderful machines in the old West Country, and time and again they have proved their reliability. In the war days they were unequalled!"

"War days?" Lena echoed. "Good lord, I had hardly finished teething, and you were still in shorts, Holmes. Tell me, Major Hardy, is Paris still on the Seine?"

She was bored with airplanes.

Somehow they denoted tragedy.

She would never forget the horror of the morning.

"Paris is a city of change," Hardy replied. "Bohemian life has moved from north to south, from Montmartre to Montparnasse. The Paris of the hotels is moving westwards. Already the Parc Monceau is old-fashioned, while the most fashionable hotels are at the Etoile. As for the theatres, there is a public demand now for reform. Prices will have to be cheaper, the intervals not so long, and the seats much more comfortable. Paris is moving with the times, my dear Miss Somerton!"

So Hardy knew his Paris!

Holmes frowned.

Dacre sent Hardy a keen glance.

"That means," he said casually, "you have many interests in the French capital?"

Hardy was non-committal.

His bluish-grey eyes narrowed.

A scowl appeared on his face.

"I go to Paris when the mood comes," he said philosophically. "I fly on to Berlin when I tire of Paris. I even fly as far as Japan, but that is when I am bored with Paris and Berlin. Then when the Berliners tempt me to suicide I come back to Vienna." He gave a disjointed laugh, but there was no mirth in it.

Lena shivered.

A laugh like that seemed to come from the jungle.

Was Hardy a consummate actor?

"Well, here is the police car," Dacre announced. "What is the programme, friends? Do we all go to Mountdale, and lunch with Major Hardy, or do you return to the hotel, Miss Somerton? What about that call to the sub-editorial Chief?"

Lena accepted her cue.

She coloured slightly and glanced at Holmes.

He was pleading with all his might.

"Yes," she answered promptly, "I must hurry back and report to Fleet Street. Major, I am sure I am delighted to meet you. One day soon perhaps you will invite me to Mountdale?"

The furry cap was doffed.

"Nothing will give greater pleasure," he answered. "Journalists are rather a nuisance, Miss Somerton, but that does not apply to you. Amongst the gods you are favoured."

Holmes gave a formal salute.

"Au revoir, Major!" he said gaily. "Don't blaze up your next bus until I have a flip on it. I expect the Air Force will certify me insane, but if not there is a chance I may fly again. Take care of yourself."

Lena took charge at the wheel, and soon the car was out of sight.

The distance to Mountdale was comparatively short.

Dacre and Hardy made a sharp turning to the left, and in ten minutes they entered the large gates of the mansion.

The Yard man was impressed with the scene.

Mountdale was built on modern lines, and the bold sweep of carriage drive gave it a pronounced dignity. The building was a dream of architectural beauty. It somewhat resembled the French villas found in Paris Plage, except that the design was entirely English, while in that respect it was unique. Mountdale had stepped out of the traditional.

As for the lawns, flower-gardens, and vast expanse of terrace, these all came into the delightful scheme of things, making Mountdale the most picturesque mansion in that part of the country.

They walked slowly up the drive.

Hardy still smoked the cigarette.

Strange how he postponed the murder details!

"You never married?" Dacre asked.

"No, like yourself I am a celibate. I do not object to the sex, but marriage has never appealed to me. Of course, my friend, a ravishing girl like Lena Somerton is vastly different!"

Dacre paused to light a cigar.

Then he switched on to the two crimes.

All the time he watched his companion.

"Good heavens," Hardy exclaimed at the finish, "I never heard anything so revolting in my life. You say all this happened at Cottingdale, and that the bodies were actually flung from the machine. Good lord, Dacre, it's the most ghastly business I have known. Stabbed them to death and drank their blood! Ghoulish, bestial, wolfish! No wonder you wished to borrow my plane. You will have the new one immediately it arrives. I shall assist you to the greatest extent in my power."

Dacre listened to him in silence.

Was Hardy sincere or merely acting?

There was something forced about his concern.

"I may not trouble you after all," Dacre continued. "Headquarters have promised to send down a machine, and I am told it will reach Cottingdale at any moment. But I wanted one an hour ago. It might have made all the difference in the world."

The mansion was reached, and they mounted the white terrace steps together.

Dacre was enchanted with everything.

There were unmistakable signs of wealth.

A uniformed butler stood at the door.

"Come right inside," Hardy requested. "I left instructions I would get back for lunch, but a burning airplane was not in my calculation. However, we can manage some food for you. No need to go back to the hotel for the present. I am proud to have you at Mountdale, Dacre, for I have read most of your adventures, and I rather envy your brain power. I presume this will be regarded as your biggest problem?"

"It all depends," Dacre replied. "I never worry about that part of it. To every mystery there is a solution, and often the Fates are kind. Even airplane murderers have their weak moments, and I am a great believer in Fate."

They had entered the magnificent library.

It appalled Dacre with its immensity.

Never had he seen such a multitude of books.

There was a short interval during which Hardy had a chat with his housekeeper. He told her briefly what happened, and she was overjoyed at his escape. Tidings of the accident had reached the servants, but they had been discretion itself. At all cost the Major must not be worried. His temper was bound to have a terrific reaction, and they knew what that meant! Yes, so long as the Major was safe in body and limb, the housekeeper was indifferent to anything else. Lunch would be served in fifteen minutes.

"Yes, Fate plays a stupendous part," Hardy agreed, as he returned to the library. "I don't believe in charms, for instance, but I wear that small ivory cross on my watch-chain. There it is, Dacre. I purchased that in a second-hand shop in

Italy. The old gent was an anti-Fascist, but Mussolini never heard about it, and that cross I would not sell for a thousand pounds!"

Dacre examined the curio gravely.

He turned it slowly over.

Hardy's initials were on the back.

"How long have you carried that about with you?" he asked quietly.

"Since I purchased my first plane two years ago. It has proved a real friend, Dacre, and I have asked my solicitor to put it in my coffin. Now that's the only talisman I possess. What's yours?"

Dacre allowed himself a slow smile.

"I put my faith in the stars," he said modestly. "A talisman has no attraction for mc. Perhaps that is because they are so numerous, but I must say I admire your cross. Let us hope your luck continues!"

Was Dacre getting a trifle cynical?

He was glancing round the room with renewed interest.

Once again he was struck by its tremendous size.

"Ah," sighed Hardy, "that is my one weakness, Dacre. I am passionately fond of books. I brought back six with me from a Paris stall, and now they are all ashes."

The maid entered at that instant.

"A police-inspector to see Mr. Dacre," she announced.

Dacre rose at once.

"Pardon me a moment, Hardy," he said swiftly. "No need to invite him inside. Perhaps it is only a message from the Station!"

He passed into the hall.

Inspector Murray stood in the doorway.

He gave a smart salute.

"Something important, Mr. Dacre," he said quickly. "This has been found near the airplane. Thought you would like to see it. The machine has burnt itself out. This must have fallen from the plane, sir."

Dacre caught hold of it.

It was a young lady's handbag!

CHAPTER XI

A POSTPONED LUNCH

"HAVE YOU looked inside?"

"Yes, sir. But there is nothing but a silk handkerchief and a powder puff!"

Dacre gave the Inspector a hard stare.

"How near the machine did you find it?"

"About ten yards, sir. And when you examine it, Mr. Dacre, you will see it is slightly singed. It must have fallen out when the machine nose-dived. The crowd rushed forward to examine the plane, but Constable Tillotson and I kept them back. I then picked up that bag from the ground."

A powder-puff!

Always a woman in some tragedy.

Dacre almost smiled.

"Thank you, Murray," he said quietly. "I am very glad you acted so promptly. I have already mentioned your name to the Chief Constable. Just keep on as you are doing and it will mean promotion. As regards the bag, leave it with me and keep silent. You understand?"

The Inspector saluted and withdrew.

Dacre returned to the library.

Apparently the owner of Mountdale had not moved.

"That was a police Inspector," Dacre observed. "He has an interesting habit of picking up things, and this hand-bag he found near your plane. He says it must have fallen from the machine. Rather awkward for you, Major, but he spotted it ten yards from the plane, and he was the only individual near the machine. Rather a clever find on his part, isn't it, but possibly you may be annoyed at his clear vision. He has certainly no need to wear glasses!"

Hardy took the bag in his hand.

He did so with a curious reluctance.

Then his teeth parted in a brilliant smile.

"Mother of saints," he exclaimed "I bought that bag in Paris for my cousin. She lives in Welwyn Garden City, and her birthday is next Thursday. Not exactly a costly gift, but I am always at a loss to know what a woman wants."

"I often find myself in that predicament," Dacre vouchsafed. "But you are quite sure you bought that bag in Paris, Major?"

"I am absolutely positive!"

Dacre took the bag back in his hand.

He hated all feminine objects like the devil.

But this one made his dark eyes flash.

"Don't be too sure," he counselled. "For instance, look! Inside the bag is a handkerchief and a powder-puff. Really, Major, I feel you are pulling my leg. Or does it mean you bought those two items as well? What a comprehensive brain you must have?"

Hardy floundered and frowned.

He looked painfully embarrassed.

A venomous glint entered his blue-grey eyes.

"It means nothing of the kind," he roared. "Darnation fury, I am an idiot, a hopeless goat, an imbecile! I have lifted the wrong bag in mistake!"

"What a stupendous error," Dacre sympathised. "But there is still an element of comedy. Do Paris shopkeepers sell bags in that fashion? Or is there a terrible shortage of brown paper in France?"

Major Hardy was decidedly uncomfortable.

A word escaped him that cannot be printed.

The situation was extremely delicate.

"My God," he groaned, "don't you understand when a man's bluffing? Dacre, I am not an archangel. Listen to my tale of woe. I met a charming young mademoiselle in Paris—ah, those delicious young creatures—and she consented to come for a plane-ride! But alas, she suffered from a sudden attack of air-sickness, and the little flip came to an end in twenty minutes. She begged to be excused, she pleaded for me to land, and I sent her home in a taxi. The hand-bag she left behind, and when I saw it in the plane, I thought she had left it for me intentionally. It would give me an excuse to call at her address. But there was no card inside, and in desolation I retained the bag as a memoir of a vast disappointment!"

Dacre groaned in sympathy.

It was a most deplorably sad story!

Unfortunately the Yard man could not weep.

"The young lady was French, you say?"

"Good lord, yes! Why do you ask?"

"Because this bag was manufactured in England!"

Hardy glared at him.

"Dacre, you are joking!"

"No, I am in deadly earnest, Major. Look, the name and address stamped on the lining. Now let me give you a real thrill. Would you be very much astonished if I put you under arrest?"

Hardy gasped.

"Good heavens, you don't think—" he began. The pained protest on his face was pathetic He looked a picture of sublime indignation. The blue-grey eyes were filled with anguish.

Dacre regarded him with cynical amusement.

"Never leave a dramatic sentence like that unfinished," he warned. "Go on, Major, make a breast of it."

"Make a breast of it!" Hardy exclaimed in the wildest consternation. "Good Saint Michael, you don't imagine I am concerned in those crimes!"

Dacre shrugged his shoulders.

What game was he playing?

Was Hardy nothing but a consummate actor?

"Well, you certainly enter the category of a suspect," Dacre declared.

Hardy tottered to the nearest chair.

"My God, you have nothing against me," he pleaded. "All you have got is just a shadow of circumstantial evidence. All you have discovered is a woman's handbag and a ghastly powder-puff! What are you going to make out of those?"

Dacre found space for the hand-bag in his pocket.

"Don't be illogical," he coaxed. "I accuse you of nothing, my dear man. I simply infer that the evidence against you is black. Well, a dull brown at least! You might, for instance—had you been a bold, naughty man—have planned that plane bonfire! It might be regarded as a clever move. It may have contained reddish marks—the colour of blood, perhaps—and difficult to wipe out. And one might think almost that the handbag put you in Queer Street. But there is nothing to worry about. All you have to do, Major, is to tell the golden truth. Who was your French mademoiselle? Incidentally, where would a French telegram find her?"

Hardy groaned in spirit.

He was in the very devil of a mess.

How the blazes could he extricate himself?

"But this is an affair of honour," he protested. "Besides, I cannot give you the girl's name. The young girl I picked up belonged to Montmartre, and I met her on the outskirts by accident. If you want the truth, I made a stupendous mistake. She was not the gay Parisienne I imagined, and I was annoyed at my terrible blunder. When she became air-sick that finished it. Believe it or not, that is the truth, and the whole truth."

Dacre gave a low whistle.

He stared at a famous oil-painting.

It was a Rembrandt and apparently an original.

"My dear Hardy," he protested, "I have never doubted your good faith a moment. I have merely placed you in an imaginary predicament. What I point out is that English hand-bag, which places you in a difficult position, but then I forgot to tell you something, and that leaves a loophole in your favour. I happen to know, you see, that English hand-bags are sold in Paris, so your mistake may simply have been one of nationality! Perhaps that is why I have not placed you under arrest, or is it just because I have an unspeakably kind heart?"

Hardy wiped his forehead with his sleeve.

It was a vulgar action, but it expressed his relief.

He emitted a ponderous sigh.

"Good lord, Dacre, you have almost spoilt our lunch," he groaned. "I do wish you would not play a practical joke of this kind. Why, you have given me quite a fright. I thought landing in a parachute was a big enough thrill for one day! But what about a cocktail? Come, a dry Martini, or a special vermouth made by my butler. Saunders is an absolute expert on mixed drinks. Try one for heaven's sake."

Dacre glanced at his watch.

"No," he said, "I must tender you an apology. I have forgotten something, Major, and it must have my immediate attention. Besides, I deserve to be shot. You look white and tired, and what you really want is a good rest. I was a brute to intrude in this fashion. No, I must return at once to the 'White Hart' Hotel, but perhaps in a few days I will look you up. I am the very devil for springing a surprise!"

Hardy shrugged his shoulders.

He also glanced up at the Rembrandt.

It seemed to be smiling in approval.

"Well, have it your own way," he replied. "I certainly intend to have a bath and a good sleep. That English Channel crossing was none too pleasant, and the parachute stunt gave me a nasty twinge. What an eternity of waiting before the blasted thing opened! Yet it was only a few seconds! . . . You are surely not going to keep that handbag?"

Dacre stared at a Japanese curio on a small table.

Then his eyes roamed over the multitudinous books.

Finally he glanced at the rich, red carpet.

"I fear I must disappoint you in that respect," he rejoined. "You see, Hardy, we damned Yard men are so cursedly inquisitive. For instance, before I leave, may I ask one or two harmless queries?"

"Why, of course, man!"

"My Chief would like to know your business in Paris, how long you stayed in the French capital, and what was your address in the City of Pleasure? You did not carry that plane in your pocket, so what was the nearest aerodrome, and where did you lodge the machine? Absolutely ridiculous questions, my dear Hardy, but just the kind that London Chief will ask. Can you tell me what to tell him?"

Hardy drew a deep breath.

Then he rose to his feet.

Both hands he thrust in his pockets.

"Curse every detective that was ever born," he said sadly. "Well, Dacre, you are not a bad Yard specimen, so I will take you into confidence, but not a word to the papers! I am interested in a new French railway syndicate—well, to the extent of several thousand pounds—and my visit concerned that project. My abode of love was the '*Hotel Carillon*' in the *Bois de Ventome*, and you will find my name in the register. I have written it with a firm hand to prove my sobriety. As for the plane, it was lodged at Le Touquet aerodrome, for the French hotels will not permit an airplane in a bedroom! One day and one night I stayed in the French capital—and then that dear, charming mademoiselle!"

Dacre grinned and moved to the door.

The Rembrandt appeared to grin also.

It certainly smirked.

"Well, dear boy," he said sadly, "I will not detain you another moment. If I find those details correct, I may drop you a postcard, and let you know, but if I find any flaw in that fairy story, remember I shall turn out the villain of the piece."

Hardy accompanied him to the terrace steps.

Nothing could have been more wonderful than his farewell.

He gripped the detective's hand hard.

"You and I are going to be real friends," he declared. "Remember this, Dacre: I bear you not the slightest ill-will. I think you are perfectly justified in your remarks, but for heaven's sake do not keep a single suspicion in your mind. I have a perfectly clear alibi, and you have only got to verify it. When you do, I shall have great happiness in accepting your apology."

He turned to his butler.

"My chauffeur and the car!" he ordered. "Have Mr. Dacre driven at once to the 'White Hart' Hotel, and tell Robertson to make it snappy!"

So ten minutes later Dacre was transported to the Cottingdale hotel. There he found the others at lunch, and he was just in time to join them. They listened eagerly to what happened at Mountdale!

Lena examined the bag for herself.

Even the powder-puff claimed her attention.

She also scrutinised the handkerchief for initials.

"Now this would make an excellent story for the *Sentinel*," she announced, "but, of course, Dacre, you will censor that at once. Yet as I must give the news about the burning plane, your interview with Hardy would be deemed a sensation."

The expert commenced his luncheon.

He was feeling exceedingly well-pleased.

Perhaps he had landed on a real pointer at last!

"My dear girl," he answered, "you were born without a single ounce of tact. To talk about Hardy would not be policy at present, and the merest hint of suspicion would spoil my plans. I have merely shown you that handbag out of pure cussedness. I knew it would excite your feminine curiosity, and possibly you might make some original remark, but once again you have dismally failed me. As regards our mysterious friend Hardy, leave him to me. I have him placed in his proper category, and believe me, he is something less than a damned fool! His movements in France will be confirmed through my Paris agent, and a cable will reach me before midnight. Rest assured, he will be kept under observation. Chief Constable Muir has had a phone message from me already!"

Holmes glanced across with admiration.

He realised that Dacre had a master mind.

The famous detective always retained an ace.

"All the same," Holmes remarked, leaning across the table, "the Major's story sounds fishy! I know the gay Parisiennes as well as Hardy, and believe me, they don't glide about with British handbags! No, they prefer something more chic, something more alluringly feminine! Miss Somerton, you won't call me a liar!"

Lena gave a little smile.

"I rather fancy you are right," she agreed. "That is not the bag a mademoiselle would carry. It is too dignified and Anglo-Saxon. As for the powder-puff, it shows remarkably good taste, but it is unmistakably English. Major Hardy, I am afraid, is a bad egg. He has never been taught to say his prayers. He is really a bold, wicked man!"

Dacre replaced the bag in his pocket.

He turned to Holmes.

That individual was all attention.

"My friend," he observed, "you will be able to help. My Yard Chief is sending me down a Government plane. I hope to heaven it does not crash like the other two, but it should reach Cottingdale at any moment, and the pilot will land near the police station. P.C. Gutteridge has been told to look out for it, but I want you to see after the machine until I get back. I go down this afternoon to Weymouth, and if the fates are kind, I may stay all night at Claridge's Hotel. But a plane is slightly different to a valise. One can't drag it about all over the place, and Cottingdale seems a very convenient spot for it."

Holmes clapped his hands.

"Splendid fellow," he answered. "No need to worry over that point, Dacre. I am your man every time. I will find a suitable shed for it, and see that it is properly looked after. My fee will be five guineas per hour, and one penny on the bottle. Besides, when you are speaking again to headquarters, just mention you have engaged me as your assistant pilot. If you start chasing that air villain all over the show, you will want a free hand for a revolver."

"Not a bad idea," Dacre echoed. "We will see how things work out. But don't start giving Gutteridge joy-rides, otherwise he is going to be sick and I'm going to be angry!"

"Why the Cottingdale area?" Lena mused. "Why has it been selected for these terrible crimes?"

Lunch with her had been somewhat of a pretence. She had not recovered from the shock of the morning!

"To that there is only one logical answer," Dacre replied. "Cottingdale happens to be close to Weymouth, and a country district is less likely to attract attention. By the way, Miss Somerton, I start in my car for Weymouth at three o'clock. You can come along with me if you like. I am going to interview that Mary Brookes, the girl friend of the first victim. Afterwards you can secure rooms in the town, and post me your address to Claridge's Hotel. I presume you have told Holmes about the decoy plan."

"Heavens, yes!" Holmes butted in. "Lena and I are almost as intimate as man and wife. There, I have put my foot in it again. A thousand pardons, Miss Somerton. I mean we are just entering the David-Jonathan stage, eternal friends and that sort of thing. But anything like a flirtation is taboo. That beastly murder spoilt things."

Lena jumped suddenly to her feet.

Luncheon had come to an end.

She was looking remarkably lovely.

"I almost forgot," she exclaimed. "I must run along and interview dear old Gutteridge. Then I am going to have a chat with Inspector Murray and the Chief Constable himself. Gee whiz, if I can't make them sit up in Fleet Street, I will resign before breakfast tomorrow."

She paused.

Dacre was staring at her in provoking fashion.

She gave a wonderful smile and ran from the room.

CHAPTER XII

WHO SPOKE TO RUTH HENDERSON?

THE POLICE car raced along the Weymouth road.

Lena controlled the steering-gear.

Dacre sat beside her in a strange silence.

He reflected on his interview with Major Frank Hardy. He thanked his stars he went to Mountdale, because although he had found no evidence against Hardy, he made a discovery that was of stupendous importance. It brought him in contact with the biggest thing in his career, and when he unravelled the mystery to the last thread, Fleet Street would pronounce it the biggest sensation since the Armistice. But his lips would remain sealed for the present. He could take no one into confidence. Yet when he made an arrest no one would be more surprised than the murderer himself.

"Good lord," Lena gasped, "it's like driving one's uncle home from a funeral. Dacre, do you know you haven't spoken since we left Cottingdale? What is preying on your mind? Have you forgotten to tip the head waiter, or are you working out some big problem? If you have solved the mystery to those murders, remember that I am a poor working journalist. That is where I want to shine."

The Yard man lit a cigarette.

This girl contributed to his amusement.

She possessed the knack of being desperately original.

"I promise you the solution before the end of the chapter," he replied. "For a few days, I must remain dumb. I admit that is a pity so far as you are concerned, but I could never trust a woman with anything vital."

Lena smiled in the most provocative fashion.

Never did she look more beautiful.

The colour in her cheeks was heavenly.

"Oh, nincompoop," she sighed, "why did I not remain behind with Holmes! He at least would have put his arm round me, and prevented me falling out of this car. Yet I am not sure that I like him. I have come to the conclusion he is an incorrigible flirt."

"That thought has occurred to me also," Dacre confessed.

Lena's blue eyes reminded him of the Mediterranean.

Then he shivered.

He must not turn sentimental at all cost!

"You are perfectly certain you are not jealous?"

She leaned close to him, a trifle closer than was really necessary, for he was possessed of good hearing, but she loved to tease this man. Woman-haters she adored! But he must never guess the extent of her admiration.

"Jealous? No, not the least little crumb!"

The car slowed gradually down.

Dacre fumed with impatience.

This was getting beyond a joke.

"Why are we stopping?" he enquired. He was feeling bored with the vagaries of this girl. Yes, he had made a mistake to bring her. He should have left her behind with Holmes or the hotel manager. He should have put her under the care of P.C. Gutteridge!

"But we are not stopping," she protested. "You have made a slight error of judgment. We are just slowing down so that I may admire the scenery. I can see nothing else to interest me, and I find the scowl on your face so nauseating. Do you hate me very much?"

Dacre took the cigarette from his mouth.

He stared at the girl in amazement.

She returned his gaze unmoved.

"Hate you?" he echoed. "Of course I hate every member of your species, but it happens to be a generalised hate, so do not take that as a personal insult. If you had told me you were going to discuss sentimental values of this kind—"

Lena sniffed and sent the car on with a rush.

She realised the man was a goof!

In her case, she decided the hate element was entirely personal. She loathed Dacre with all her heart. She ranked him as the most impossible man in the whole of creation. No, she would not admit one single good attribute. He represented nothing but a bumptious, swollen-headed, sophisticated—Words failed her!

"Didn't you know I was pulling your leg?" she retorted. "Gee, Dacre, you never understand when you are being fooled. But look, here we are on the outskirts of Weymouth. Where does that Mary Brookes live? Ah yes, I remember. 19 Harcourt Street, fourth turning to the left. We will soon find it."

Three minutes later they arrived.

They were lucky to find the girl at home.

"She has cried her eyes out all day," said her mother to Dacre, leading the detective and Lena into the sitting-room. "Just a second and I will send her in to you." Dacre had already explained the object of his visit.

When the girl friend of Ruth Henderson entered the room, Dacre noted she was in great distress. She burst into a fresh torrent of tears, and Lena did her utmost to console her. She also was moved to a great feeling of pity, for she remembered that second horror of the morning, and knew she stood in the centre of drama. Mary Brookes was led to the nearest chair, and Dacre added his own personal words of comfort. Much as he hated the sex, he was always profoundly affected by a woman's tears. He saw this girl was just about twenty-two years old, that she was a decent type of Weymouth factory-worker, and that character was stamped on her face. She wore a black dress in memory of her friend.

"I promise only to ask a few questions," Dacre observed. "They may not help a great deal, Miss Brookes, but on the other hand, you may make some casual remark of vital importance. I take it you are very anxious to assist. I have been sent from the Yard to investigate the murder of your friend, so please do not keep a single thing back. Just give me as much detail as possible."

The girl dried her eyes.

She lifted her face bravely to the detective.

She also glanced with some curiosity at Lena.

"I am a journalist on the staff of the *Sentinel*," Lena informed her, "and Mr. Dacre and I are working together. You must realise that publicity in this case is going to count, Miss Brookes, because the fiend who murdered your friend may be planning another crime!" They thought it prudent not to mention that a second murder had already occurred. They had no wish to give this girl hysteria, and already she bordered on a state of panic.

"Very well," Mary Brookes replied, "I will tell you anything you want to know. I knew Ruth Henderson all those years—since we left school, in fact—and I only wish I was dead with her. I have no other friend in the world. She was the one friend who mattered, the one girl in that factory whom I could trust. Now she's murdered! . . . Mr. Dacre, promise you will find the brute who did that thing. Promise!" . . . She broke into a fresh fit of crying, and Dacre turned away his own head. He saw the tears for the first time in the eyes of Lena Somerton, and he was strangely affected by the sight.

"We are going to do our best," he promised. "But we are searching for some description of the man, and we want to see if you can put us on the track. I have already had a chat with Mr. Henderson, and I expect he has seen you last night, but he could not give us any information. Now here is my first question, Miss Brookes. When you were out walking with your friend last week did you speak about an airplane trip to anyone, or did any person make such a suggestion to you? Now think well please before you answer. That is very important!"

The girl shook her head with great emphasis.

"No, Mr. Dacre," she replied, "we never spoke to anyone about an airplane, and no one ever mentioned one to us. I do know that Ruth was much interested in flying. She often stopped in the street to watch them pilots and their monkey-tricks, and often we have seen them stunting and looping. But nothing else."

Dacre gave a comprehensive nod.

He realised the girl was excited.

She had spoken rather too quickly.

"When was the last air carnival held in Weymouth?" he asked.

"About two months ago, but Ruth and I did not go to that. We went that week-end to some friends in Portland. That is how I remember."

Dacre folded his arms.

"Those air carnivals are getting pretty frequent. There are also one or two flying clubs in the vicinity. Had you ever a letter from one of those clubs, Miss Brookes, or did you ever hear your friend mention such a communication? I am just wondering, you see, if Miss Henderson accepted any offer unknown to you—the offer of a free trip in an airplane, for instance?"

The girl shook her head.

"I never saw any such letter," she declared, "and I am positive Ruth never received one. She would have told me about it at once. We shared all secrets. If a man as much as winked at her, she would tell me and we would laugh over it. Ruth and I were lifelong friends. Can you realise what that means?" Her voice trailed off to another sob. Her whole body shook with some powerful emotion.

Lena glanced across at Dacre.

The questions seemed to be leading nowhere.

Nothing was being gained.

"And when you finished business in the factory, what did you do with yourselves in the evening? The usual programme, I suppose? Cinemas, or a walk, or some sewing?"

"Exactly, Mr. Dacre. We both loved the pictures, and we went twice a week. No settled nights, just when we felt like it, and at other times we went a walk, or stayed at home and did house-work . . . That is why I will miss Ruth so much."

"No settled nights for pictures, but about those walks, Miss Brookes? I am rather curious about what happened last week. Try and fix your mind on these last six days. What was the last evening you went for a walk, and in what direction did you go?"

Mary did not hesitate.

Her brown eyes glowed for an instant.

She would never forget her last walk with her friend.

"We took our last walk on Friday evening," she answered. "I could not bear to think of pictures that night, so we went a stroll along the Pier, Mr. Dacre. We took a seat out near the bandstand, and watched the sunset for hours. The band was playing, of course, and Ruth declared it was the loveliest evening she ever spent. We got talking about old times, you see, and—"

Dacre interrupted.

"Now one moment, please!" he begged. "From the time you left the house with your friend that Friday evening, Miss Brookes, until you returned home late at night, were you or your friend accosted by a single man?"

Mary thought hard.

She pressed a hand to her forehead.

She was endeavouring to concentrate.

"We are often spoken to by young men, Mr. Dacre," she confessed, "but we have never taken the slightest notice of them. Ruth and I have always been afraid of marriage because we were such staunch friends, and we dreaded anything coming between that friendship. I am positive no one spoke to us that night. No man, I mean. We were just remarking how peaceful the evening had been, for often we have been worried by these holiday-makers, chaps who think that every girl can be picked up for a smile."

Dacre was not defeated.

He had one last question.

It was more important than all the rest.

"I am going to stake a lot on this last query," he said with a reassuring smile. "Now remember, Miss Brookes, we are dealing with Friday evening. I want you to fix all your thoughts on that night, and to realise that your answer may vitally help in the solution of this mystery. Here is my question. You have just told us that not a single man addressed you or your friend that evening, that you spent a few glorious hours on the Weymouth pier, listened to the band, and then strolled homewards. But did anyone speak to Ruth Henderson that evening? A woman, for instance?"

Lena gasped.

She saw the dreadful significance of the query.

She was almost frightened by it.

"A woman?" Mary Brookes repeated in a hoarse voice. Then she rose slowly to her feet. She, too, possessed an inkling of what the detective meant. Her features turned white for an instant. Her lips trembled. "Yes, Mr. Dacre, a woman spoke to Ruth at the corner of the Esplanade, just before we strolled on the Pier, but it was merely to ask the whereabouts of some street. At least that was the impression I got, for I walked on while Ruth spoke to her, thinking at first it was some woman friend. She told me afterwards what the woman wanted!"

Dacre gave a dramatic nod.

He leaned slightly forward.

His dark eyes glowed.

"That was the deduction I made," he said earnestly. "A woman spoke to your friend, detained her a few minutes, and then let her go. Is that what happened?"

"Yes, Mr. Dacre."

"Now think hard again. Could you describe that woman, Miss Brookes? Could you recognise her again? Could you give me any outstanding detail about her so that I might get on her track?"

The girl was puzzled.

She half-dreaded to speak.

She looked at the Yard man in a dazed way.

"What does he mean?" she said to Lena. "That woman had nothing to do with the murder. She had lost her way and wanted to find some address. What harm was there in her speaking to Ruth!"

Lena patted her hand gently.

"Don't you see," she coaxed, "that may have been a man in disguise, Miss Brookes! Mr. Dacre and I have known such things to happen. It is not the first time a man has personated a woman—for his own evil purpose, of course—and that is what may have happened on Friday night."

"Precisely," Dacre stressed. "No one takes much notice of a woman stopping another woman in the street. If that was a man as I imagine it to be, we do not know what plan may have been in his mind. He may have watched you and your friend for many nights, he may have been attracted towards her in some fashion, and he was anxious to get acquainted with her. He may have met your friend again the following morning, still dressed in the same female disguise, and Miss Henderson, unsuspecting, may have been led into an ambush. For all we know, the disguise may have been worn in the plane itself. There are women pilots, you know, Miss Brookes. My friend here can manage a plane, and there are countless others. Miss Henderson may have had no scruples where a woman was the pilot, and she may have had no time to communicate with you. Do you see my point? Do you see why I am so anxious to trace that woman who spoke to Ruth Henderson on Friday night?"

Mary Brookes was appalled by the ghastliness of it all.

Yet she pulled herself together.

She saw a chance of helping the detective.

"My God, you may be right!" she faltered "That may be the real explanation of it all, Mr. Dacre. Well, I should certainly know that woman again. We did not see her again that night, but I would be able to recognise her anywhere. She did strike me as rather peculiar, although I did not pay much attention at the time. She wore a dark green dress, I remember, a rather funny shaped hat, and a small black veil stopping short at the nose. She was rather tall, and walked very slowly."

Dacre rose to his feet.

"If you can recognise that woman," he said gravely, "you will do me a tremendous favour, Miss Brookes. Now listen, please, to this suggestion. When you want to get hold of me, go direct to the nearest police-station, and you will soon discover where I am to be found. I may stay to-night at Claridge's Hotel, Weymouth, and to-morrow I may put up at the 'White Hart' Hotel, Cottingdale. If you run across that woman any day this week, try and follow her to her destination, get hold of her address at all cost, and ask the police to help you in your task. Then, when you have made that discovery, get in touch with me at once. Do you understand?"

"Perfectly, Mr. Dacre," the girl replied with great fervour. "I will certainly do as you ask. I won't go near the factory this week. I will spend every day looking for that woman. I believe I have seen her about the Esplanade once or twice—not since Friday, of course—but I may run across her again, and I will watch where she goes. I will follow her for miles."

Lena intervened at that instant.

"And I am going to help you in your task," she said with a wonderful smile. "Leave Miss Brookes in my care, Dacre. She and I will arrange to meet each other, and if she can point that woman out to me, I will see that she is followed while my friend here gets hold of a constable. Do I understand you wish the woman detained until you arrive at the station?"

Dacre shook his head.

"Try and leave the constable out of it," he counter-suggested. "What I want is the address of the woman, but if that is impossible to obtain, then you may ask the police to detain her. You see, I want to spring a surprise. Recollect also that the woman may be perfectly genuine, but I have a suspicion that something is wrong. Ruth Henderson would not have been gulled by a man, but she might have been deceived by a woman, and that makes all the difference."

Mary Brookes sank back in the nearest chair.

The tears came again in a mighty torrent.

Dacre, ever-human, spoke to Lena.

"Stay with her a little and make your plans," he suggested. "That idea of yours is excellent, Miss Somerton, and when you want me, you know where I am to be found."

Lena gave him a bright smile.

"My dear man," she answered, "don't think you are going to steal a march on me in that fashion. I will do as you ask with pleasure, but as there was no law in England to prevent me sleeping overnight at the 'White Hart,' Cottingdale, all the brilliant detectives in the world won't prevent me staying at Claridge's Hotel, Weymouth. That is where I am going to dine to-night, friend Dacre, and you will find my name in the hotel register, also the number of my room if you want to treat me to dinner."

CHAPTER XIII

THE MYSTERY WOMAN

THE MIRACLE really happened.

Lena dined that night at Claridge's Hotel, Weymouth.

As usual, she looked incomparably lovely.

"Now, look here, young lady," Dacre cautioned, "I want to put you wise about one or two points. You have heard me speak of M. Cambon, the distinguished member of the French *Sûreté*? Well, I am expecting him to reach this hotel at any moment. He is supposed to be staying here on holiday, but I rather fancy he has other fish to fry—!"

"You mean, he is hunting down some criminal?"

"I mean nothing for the present, but you need not run away when he does come. You will find him a volcanic personage, and I am not sure whether you will like him. He has no respect for man, woman, or beast. But his status in Paris cannot be ignored, and I find it best to humour him. He has manifested an interest in this case, and this second crime must have given him another thrill. I am anxious to hear his observations, but say nothing to him about the mystery-woman, Major Hardy, or the girl Mary Brookes. To do that, you see, might upset my plans."

Lena gave a radiant smile.

She quite understood.

Professional jealousy, of course.

"Thanks for the hint, Dacre," she declared. "I simply adore Frenchmen, however, so if the great Monsieur Cambon deigns to notice a poor girl journalist, I may fall in love with him at first sight. Yes, you mentioned the famous Frenchman, and so did P.C. Gutteridge, with words I am not likely to forget. I fear Gutteridge does not like your French colleague, my friend. Indeed he went so far as to declare him an ass. He even hinted that M. Cambon has escaped from a French lunatic asylum, and I have promised to make some enquiry in that respect. Poor old Gutteridge. He gave me a headache laughing, and in the end he offered me a nip of brandy."

Dacre smiled.

The dinner was proving a success.

He felt distinctly pleased.

"Gutteridge is a man that Dickens would have immortalised," he observed. "As regards M. Cambon, I fear he is not to be despised. Between ourselves, I am not overwhelmed with his personality, but I never forget that French word '*diplomatique*.' You see, I am indebted to the *Sûreté* for many favours, and one must be polite to its members. By the way, I have got in touch with the Weymouth Police Superintendent, and have circulated a description of the mystery-woman who spoke to Ruth Henderson. I have also phoned the same message to the Yard, and hope my efforts will have some definite result. I want to get on the track of that individual."

Lena burst into another laugh.

"Yes, you always did hate women," she reminded him, "and now that particular individual will be first on the list. Supposing my friend, she was really a woman?"

"In that case," he answered with a smile "there would be rational ground for my hate."

The dining-room was crowded.

An orchestra played faintly in a distant corner.

It was a warm August evening, and everyone seemed in gay spirits.

"What time do you meet Miss Brookes?"

"At nine o'clock to-night," Lena replied. "We will see each other at the Esplanade end of the Pier, and stroll about for an hour. We will continue these walks for a few evenings and if luck comes our way, you will have a phone message without delay. I will also move about Weymouth alone, picking up any information I can about flying men—and at the end of the week I will send you in a bill for one thousand guineas. Is that correct, Big Boy?"

Dacre ordered a special bottle of champagne.

He was impressed by those Mediterranean blue eyes.

Lena Somerton certainly deserved a good meal.

"I realise you are a very tantalising Circe," he muttered, "but I see you also know your job, and that always appeals to me. Your reward will be a tremendous scoop for the *Sentinel*, and I will see that you are privileged. But you must not try to vamp me. I promise to resist all your efforts—even after I have tasted this champagne . . . Miss Somerton, a toast to your eyes! They are far too dangerous for man's comfort, but nevertheless, I drink to them."

Lena's laugh was infectious.

She was thrilled by the romance of this dinner.

And how she hated this man.

"I think you are an angel for being kind to me," she half-whispered. "M. Cambon, Trevor Holmes, and P.C. Gutteridge can go to the devil. I raise my glass to you, Big Boy, and wish you all success in this thrilling case. But remember, I am your real mystery-woman, and I shall never be caught."

They laughed uproariously together.

Both were trying to banish the horror of the morning.

And Dacre proved himself a perfect host.

"By the way, Lena—yes, I am going to use your Christian name at odd intervals—don't, for heaven's sake, mention this mystery-woman to Fleet Street, or any member of the Press Association!"

Lena smiled back into his eyes.

The champagne coursed through her young blood.

She was feeling deliriously happy.

"Don't write me down a chump," she begged. "Good lord, I do possess three grains of grey matter. Why should you accuse me of stupidity? If you want the truth, I have simply phoned my interviews with Murray, Gutteridge, and the girl Brookes. But your mystery-woman I keep in reserve. No need to warn her in advance. I think that is your little game. Kindly pour me out another glass of that sparkling liquid—and then you may kiss me if you think no one is looking."

Dacre complied with the first request.

The temptation to carry out the second was appalling.

But he conquered.

After coffee was served, they strolled out to the lounge for a cigarette. They found rather a convenient little alcove, and had just commenced a rather intimate chat when Satan entered in the guise of M. Cambon!

"*Mon Dieu*," he exclaimed, "I have been hunting for you everywhere. Forgive my intrusion, Dacre, but the manager told me you wanted to see me the moment I arrived. I have been enjoying a quiet game of golf on the links, had a snack of dinner at a friend's house, and have just got back this instant. Now what have you got to say to me? What fresh developments have occurred, and how is the gentleman who suffers from hay fever? I mean P.C. Gutteridge!"

He was staring at Lena with undisguised admiration, and Dacre rose and performed the necessary introduction. The Frenchman bent low over the girl's hand, then took a seat opposite.

"Miss Somerton is on the staff of the *Sentinel*," Dacre added with a smile, "so anything you say, Cambon, she may use in writing against you. Be careful of these lady journalists. They always get the last word, and then they publish it . . . Well, I have news for you. I almost thought you would have heard about it. There has been a second crime . . . ."

The Frenchman paused in the act of lighting a cigarette.

His blue eyes grew round with amazement.

He gazed at Dacre with something like horror,

"What!" he exclaimed. "Have you been drinking, my friend? Are you telling me there has been another murder—a second body flung from an airplane?"

Dacre nodded.

"Nothing less than that," he sighed. "It occurred this morning after breakfast, and it completely spoilt my lunch, for I saw the last part of the tragedy with my own eyes. So did Miss Somerton, which proves that you will have to stop poking fun at poor Gutteridge. He deserves a medal and an illuminated address."

The Frenchman gasped.

He was trying hard to express his profound consternation.

His blue eyes stared.

"But *Mon Dieu*," he protested, "this thing has no precedent in history. Why, even in the war days, Dacre, we did not hurl human bodies out of airplanes! In all my career there has been nothing like it. And in the Cottingdale area! What the devil is the meaning of it? Yes, I will apologise to Gutteridge on my knees. I will even subscribe to a wreath at his funeral. He has become famous for all time, and to-morrow they will be writing about him in the *Figaro*! While your London papers—! *Tiens*, they will be ghastly during the next few days. Dacre, I offer you my professional sympathy. You are faced with the perfect crime. Not a pointer, not a solution, not a finger-mark! Is it not so?"

Lena had only uttered a few words.

She was keeping strangely quiet.

Somehow, this Frenchman was distasteful in her eyes.

"Yes," Dacre answered, "I am going to be busy, but rest assured I will get my man. I never fail, Monsieur Cambon. I always get my man!"

"I wonder!" M. Cambon muttered softly.

He threw away his cigarette and lit another.

He leaned forward.

"Let me have the details," he begged. "Describe everything that happened this morning, *mon ami*. Then I will see if I can offer any help. Perhaps I can think of something that has not occurred to you."

Dacre gave a quiet recital of the second crime.

The Frenchman listened in perfect silence.

He sat there like a stone image.

"Don't you think it all very terrible?" Lena asked for the first time. "Even now, Monsieur Cambon, we have not quite recovered from the shock. We have been trying to forget it all, making silly little jokes and drinking champagne, but I shall never forget that falling body, or what I saw afterwards—" Her voice melted away in a dry sob. She was quivering with a girlish terror. The horror of it all came back afresh!

M. Cambon expressed his complete sympathy.

"My dear young lady," he announced, "you are perfectly right. Those two crimes will stagger imagination for weeks. And it means only one thing, Dacre—that a lunatic is at large in the air. He must be caught inside a given number of hours. If not, then you know what is going to happen. Those crimes are only the beginning of a series—"

The Yard man nodded assent.

He was strangely unperturbed.

Dacre had always control of himself.

"That," he replied, "is why I am so anxious for the second victim to be identified."

Cambon stared hard.

"You have really found no pointer?" he enquired.

Dacre gazed at the tablecloth.

"Yes," he said grimly, "I am on the track of one man, and that is where you may be able to help."

The Frenchman gave a start of surprise.

Lena watched him with a critical directness.

What was coming?

"You keep me guessing," M. Cambon remarked. "Where do I come in?" He threw the girl another glance of genuine admiration, but Lena stared through him as if at a blank wall.

"I am concerned with a Major Frank Hardy," Dacre said slowly. "He lives at a place called Mountdale, out in the Cottingdale district, and he has been in possession of an airplane. He has been away from Mountdale for two days, but he returned before lunch in a dramatic manner, crashing his machine which went on fire, and escaping himself in a parachute. That man interests me profoundly, Monsieur Cambon!"

To this statement there was an astonishing sequel.

The Frenchman seemed to turn suddenly livid.

Real anger betrayed itself in every line of his face.

"What an unconscious blunder you've made," he groaned. "Good lord, Dacre, you have trespassed right on my territory. Look here, let me give you a State secret. I have allowed you to think I am here on holiday, but that is one of my tactical moves, for I have come from France to watch a big criminal. I do not know if I am watching the right man, remember, but I happen to have fastened on the individual you mention. I also am concerned in the spiritual welfare of Major Frank Hardy. Now what do you think of that for a confounded coincidence."

Dacre knocked the ash from his cigarette.

He glanced across at M. Cambon with an impassive countenance.

Then he smiled enigmatically.

"Ah, my dear Cambon, that is unfortunate," he remarked. "Now fancy two of us chasing the same hare! Two guys after one bird . . . Well, what do you wish me to do? You infer that I am trespassing? Don't you think that is putting it a trifle too strongly?"

Cambon glared at him.

"Let us stop fooling," he counselled. "Don't you see my point, Dacre? If you mess round Mountdale, and give Hardy a hint that he is under suspicion of any kind, then my goose is cooked, and Hardy won't fall into the trap that I am planning for him. I want to catch my bird in the net, but it is a little too early to ensnare him, that's all."

"What have you against him?"

"Murder. The crime was committed in Paris a month ago, and I have traced my man to the region of Cottingdale. That is why I am in Weymouth. I submit, Dacre, that my case claims precedence."

Dacre frowned.

"I cannot agree," he argued. "You may allow your man to escape, M. Cambon, but I cannot afford freedom to the one I suspect. I have no evidence against Hardy up to the present, no concrete data, I mean, but there are certain points I wish to verify, then I may act with greater decision. I am sorry, Cambon, but there is no compromise. I must keep

Hardy under observation, and I must conduct this airplane mystery as I think fit. There is my challenge."

Lena gasped.

She had listened breathlessly to every word.

Were these two famous experts going to quarrel?

Cambon lit his third cigarette.

"Well, what is it you want me to do?" he queried. "We seem to have got into a slight mess, but perhaps we can accommodate each other. How can I help, Dacre?"

The Yard man never moved.

"I should like you to get in touch with your Paris agents," he remarked. "Hardy says he is interested in some French railway syndicate, that he stayed at the *Hôtel Carillon* in the *Bois de Ventome*, and that he lodged his airplane at Le Touquet aerodrome. I am all for speed at present, and you know your Paris as I know London. I want those details confirmed at the earliest moment."

Cambon heaved a sigh.

It sounded very much like relief.

A smile touched his lips.

"That will be easy," he promised. "You will have a cable inside a few hours. The Prefect of Police in Paris is my personal friend. He will see that I am not kept waiting. It is a promise, friend Dacre, and your request I will carry out with pleasure."

Lena rose.

She glanced at her watch, and saw it was time to go.

Dacre understood.

"You two have given me an awful fright," she declared. "I really thought you were coming to blows, and I was getting ready for a first-class sensation in a Weymouth hotel, but it has all ended very tamely, and I am going to keep an appointment. Will you excuse me, gentlemen? I have to meet a friend who really must not be kept waiting."

Both men rose to their feet.

M. Cambon bowed low once again.

No one could have been more polite.

"To our next meeting," he said with a charming smile.

Dacre merely gave a friendly nod.

Then, three minutes later, a waiter came to him with an urgent message.

"A police officer to see you, Mr. Dacre, and he says it is very important."

Dacre followed the waiter to the door of the hotel.

Inspector Murray stood there with his hand at the salute.

"I have come to make a special report, sir," he began. "Have just rushed in from Cottingdale on my motor-cycle, but I knew there was not a second to be lost, and I rode like the devil—"

"Go straight ahead, Murray!"

"Well, sir, we have been watching every corner of Mountdale as you instructed, and have kept the place under observation since you left—"

"Quite right, Murray. And what has happened?"

"I have just discovered, sir, that a car left there forty minutes ago, and Constable Stevens allowed it to pass unchallenged for it only contained a woman passenger—"

"Ah!"

"But after he made his report to me, Mr. Dacre, I got a bit suspicious like, and it occurred to me that the woman might be Major Hardy disguised! Then I rang up Mountdale from the nearest house, and found he had gone to bed, and was not to be disturbed. That at least was the message from the housekeeper, but I was not quite satisfied, and so I came on here just to warn you that our man may have slipped through our hands!"

"What direction did the car take, Murray?"

"It travelled like the wind in the direction of Weymouth, sir."

"And the woman? How does the constable say she was dressed? Did he notice?"

"Yes, she wore a dark green dress, sir, a peculiar kind of hat, and a veil was pulled down over her eyes—"

CHAPTER XIV

BREAKING IT GENTLY

MONDAY MORNING brought the London papers.

Dacre made a point of reading them before breakfast.

He realised that England was stirred by the second crime.

Editors were embarrassed. They had no axe to grind against a Government Department, and they found themselves in a difficult position. It dawned on them that this was the greatest mystery-case since the War, and they confessed it was difficult to censure the Yard. That is, they knew that airplane murderers were absolutely unique, that only a short interval elapsed between the first and second crime, and that the greatest detective in England had charge of the investigation. So they contented themselves with their traditional grievance. Once again they reminded the British public that a growing number of murders remained unsolved, and they suggested a drastic change of *personnel* at Headquarters.

Dacre was tickled to death when he read that paragraph.

He thought of sending up a prayer for his Chief.

Then he decided that Sir Francis Didgett had the physical strength to pray for himself.

But the headlines were sensational. They sent a shiver of dread through every newspaper reader, and a thousand eyes were directed to any passing airplane. Imaginative people could conjure up the whole scene. A defenceless girl at the mercy of some fiendish brute in the skies, knowing that it was useless to call or shriek for help, faced with all the horror of a ghoulish lunatic! Then that sickening sequel to the ghastly crime, the drinking of the victim's blood by the murderer, and the last fatal act of hurling the human body from the airplane! Men talked about the crimes in every club; women gossiped about them in every street and doorway.

Fleet Street churned out fresh editions every half-hour.

Pictures of Cottingdale were on every front page.

And P.C. Gutteridge was photographed in every imaginable position.

Dacre perused the comments of Air Ministry officials. He read everything that appertained to the case, and although he chuckled over the growing immortality of Gutteridge, he knew that every member of the Yard looked to him to retain its prestige and find the murderer! The editor of one paper said with emphasis that no member of the Air Force was to blame. Dacre gave a distinct nod of approval. He was confident on that point already. It was within his knowledge that Whitehall officials worked furiously all through the night, sending out wireless messages in every direction, distributing telegrams to every aerodrome in the country, and he had been furnished with a report that no Government machine had gone near the Cottingdale area. That, of course, was with the exception of Holmes, who had flown a Government plane from Farnborough, but he had duly accounted for himself, and his innocence had been established. Yes, the Air Ministry officials had nothing to worry about. These two mysteries crimes did not lie at their door. Dacre was certain on that point.

He made his way to the breakfast-table, and turning to a copy of the London *Sentinel*; he read the special interviews contributed by Lena Somerton. Her photograph was also in the paper—strangely enough alongside his own—but that of course was only another coincidence. It was better than being alongside P.C. Gutteridge. Lena's articles were written with a graphic pen, and the masterly interview with P.C. Gutteridge would go down to history. But he noticed she made no reference to the little nip of brandy. He was sorry for that omission because it meant the anti-climax.

Then he glanced at his watch and saw it was eight o'clock.

What had happened to Lena?

He knew that M. Cambon had gone to London by an early train.

"Well, Big Boy, I suppose you thought I was going to sleep all day?" Lena's thrilling voice sounded in his ear, so he turned and greeted her with a smile. He was making the horrible discovery that this girl never hurried in the early hours of the morning. As a typical London journalist, used to late nights, she held to her privilege of always being late for breakfast. Yet when she made her appearance one forgot everything but her loveliness. Sleep gave her a freshness that everything else lacked, and the radiance of her blue eyes was overpowering.

"I trust I see you," Dacre said in a muffled voice. He had just commenced breakfast, and was eating a large piece of toast. He leaned across and helped himself to marmalade, then took a shy, appreciative glance at the young lady who had just accosted him.

Lena seated herself directly opposite.

It was a small table specially built for a *tête-à-tête* meal.

Dacre realised that fact with a groan of horror.

"I am not certain if you do," she answered demurely. "They say that love is blind, you know, and so far you have never made me an offer of marriage. You do really like me, Dacre, don't you? When you told me you were a woman-hater, I vowed to convert you inside a given number of hours. Tell me, for heaven's sake, that I have not failed."

"You have failed dismally," he retorted, with a sudden grab at the teapot. He felt terribly selfish this morning, and if girls arrived late in a hotel for breakfast, they must pay the inevitable penalty. "And I shall never make a member of your sex a proposal of that kind—never! So put that in your cup and drink it, you rascal. How did you get along last night, my enchantress? I suppose you had no luck of any kind? Just wandered round as if you hadn't a friend in the world. I know the stunt."

Lena sighed.

The waiter had hurried to her side.

He was carrying a fresh tray of good things!

"No," she confessed when they were alone, "we did not run across our mystery woman. But Mary Brookes and I are not going to lose heart. We realise that Weymouth is an exceptionally large town, and that a problem of this kind will not be solved in a night. Perhaps that woman will walk across our path this evening. If she does, I will see that the balloon goes up. You will be notified without delay, and that woman will be tracked to her lair. We have it all arranged."

Dacre pushed the marmalade pot across two inches.

He hated to be mean, but that was the only preserve he liked!

Then the smile returned to his face.

In a few words, he related what Murray had told him the previous evening. Lena had returned to the hotel at a late hour, and had gone straight to bed. To be perfectly truthful, she had spent the intervening time consoling Mary Brookes for the loss of her friend!

"So you see," Dacre observed, between another mouthful of toast, "we do not happen to be chasing a shadow. That odd suspicion I formed about a mystery-woman is proving correct, and Hardy has evolved into a greater enigma than ever. But one of these days he is going to experience a rude shock. He may even wish that—Never mind. Forget what I was saying."

Lena gasped.

She turned suddenly pale.

Her lips trembled.

"But why do you not make an immediate arrest?" she asked in a low voice.

"On what charge?"

"The murder of those two girls!"

Dacre expressed his disgust. Why had this supposedly-clever girl not more logic? Did she really write him down a nincompoop? Was he nothing but a blithering goat in her eyes?

"And what then?" he demanded. "After the arrest, where is the proof? If Hardy is the man I want—and mind you, I have not made a definite statement—he has thoughtfully destroyed his airplane by fire. Every scrap of criminal evidence has been eliminated. No, my lady of the pen, when I arrest a murderer, I want to see that he is hanged, and if this monster of the skies is coming into my net, then he is going to be caught red-handed. Have that last slice of toast, and pass the marmalade, please."

Lena continued the meal in a constrained silence.

She knew that Dacre was right.

If Hardy was the demon who committed those ghoulish crimes, then the detective would require absolute proof of his guilt.

"And the inquest this afternoon?" she enquired.

"I fear that will have to be postponed. I am engaged this morning on most important work—the identification of the second victim—and I have no idea how long it will last. Ah, here is a message of some kind."

It was the head waiter to say that Dacre was wanted on the telephone.

Dacre followed him at once.

It was Inspector Murray speaking from Cottingdale.

"Morning, Murray," Dacre called out, "don't tell me that Gutteridge has been poisoned."

"Something more serious than that," the Inspector laughed. "We have kept a strict watch on Mountdale, Mr. Dacre, and you will be interested to hear that Major Hardy has returned by a side entrance, but dressed in his ordinary clothes. According to the housekeeper, he went to bed yesterday afternoon, and we have been watching Mountdale ever since. I have seen Major Hardy return with my own eyes, but, acting on your instructions, I have kept out of sight and made no attempt to speak to him."

"You ought to be at the Yard, Murray," Dacre commented, "I think you have acted with wonderful intelligence. Now what time did our elusive Major return to his residence?"

"About twenty minutes ago, Mr. Dacre."

"Splendid fellow. Well, that is exactly the information I want, Murray, and let us hope he has brought his insurance card. Just keep the place under observation, but the next time try and find out where he goes and for that purpose you had better have a car handy. I am obliged for your vigilance in the matter. I shan't forget."

"There's another message from Captain Holmes, sir."

"Let's have it."

"He wants me to say that the plane is ready for your service. It reached Cottingdale at four o'clock yesterday afternoon, and has been lodged in a big empty shed belonging to a farmhouse. You will find the place only two minutes away from the station."

"Good for Holmes. Give him my kind regards, Murray, and tell him to have that engine in the pink of condition. I may want it at any moment . . . And I say, my best love to P.C. Gutteridge."

He returned to Lena and gave her the news about Hardy.

She turned pale.

The tidings left her breathless.

Was Hardy really the murderer?

"Now don't go into a panic over the gentleman," Dacre counselled. "Leave him in my care, and don't forget you may have that big scoop at any moment. Allow me to compliment you on your *Sentinel* articles. I think you are in for promotion and a month's holiday. That description of Gutteridge will go into the British Museum. I only wish Arnold Bennett had lived to read it. He would have chuckled over it for a year."

Lena tried to smile.

This airplane business was getting on her nerves.

Perhaps a nip of brandy would be really beneficial!

Dacre left the hotel after breakfast but returned in thirty minutes.

He went straight to Mr. Marcel Dupont, the hotel manager.

His face was quite grave.

There was a stern line round his lips.

"Mr. Dupont," he said gravely, "I understand that Sir Robert Anderson, the well-known London financier, is staying in this hotel. I wish to see him very urgently. Would you mind finding out if he is in the building?"

Dupont did not wait a second. He flew away to his assistant at the desk, and returned at once to the detective.

"Yes, Mr. Dacre," he said swiftly, "Sir Robert is writing letters in his own room!"

"What room is that?"

"No. 5 suite on the second landing. Shall I take you to him?"

"If you please, Dupont. I don't want to drag him down in the lift, for I have some really bad news, and he is bound to be upset."

The manager rushed the Yard man up in the elevator.

"Anything serious, Mr. Dacre?" he questioned in an awe-struck whisper.

"Very serious indeed!" was the reply.

When they reached suite No. 5 on the second door, Dupont tapped imperatively on the door. He also called out his own name, and at that the door was instantly opened.

"Come inside, Dupont," the baronet said in a pleasant voice. "What the devil is wrong? Whom have we here? Ah, Malcolm Dacre of Scotland Yard! I think I recognise you, my good fellow. Come in both of you and tell me your troubles. There are the cigars. I was just polishing off a few letters for the first mail, but they will have to stand over. Sit down, gentlemen. Make yourselves at home in my apartment."

The two men entered together, the manager closing the door.

"Yes, this is Mr. Dacre of Scotland Yard," Dupont affirmed. "I have no idea what he wants to see you about, Sir Robert, but he asked me to come along. I am afraid it is rather bad news of some kind."

The financier turned in his chair.

"Bad news?" he queried with a smile. "Well, I hope Mr. Dacre has not come to arrest me on a charge of murder! It is not as bad as that, surely?"

Dacre shook his head.

He refused to smile.

His face remained inscrutable.

"I am very pleased to meet you, Sir Robert," he said in a grave voice, "but Dupont here is quite right. I am the bearer of the most distressing news, and I hardly know how to begin."

The baronet waited patiently.

He was a short, florid type, with twinkling grey eyes, and a very shrewd face. As a financier, he was famed throughout England, and at present he was in Weymouth on a short vacation. He had been a widower for ten years, and had a large country house outside London. His town address was at Grosvenor Square.

"Well, I am waiting," he said in a hard voice. "Better let us have it, Dacre. This is not the first time I have faced bad tidings."

Dacre seemed at a complete loss.

He hated the job on hand, but there was no help for it.

He cleared his throat.

"I am sorry to tell you that your daughter has been murdered," he said quietly.

The silence was terrible.

The baronet swayed a little in his seat.

Dupont staggered to the nearest chair.

"Murdered!" Sir Robert repeated in a far-off voice. It contained not the slightest tremor. He was incapable of realisation. It was like listening to some voice on the wireless, a voice that referred to something entirely impersonal. "Murdered! I don't understand, Dacre. I am afraid you have made a blunder of some kind. Dupont, explain to him that my daughter Louise is staying in Portland with her cousin. She went there for the week-end, and, so far as I know, is perfectly safe . . . There has been some stupendous mistake."

The hotel manager rose to his feet.

He was acting in blind obedience to the command.

He approached the detective in an awestruck manner.

"Louise Anderson is with her cousin in Portland," he repeated in a low voice. "I know that for a fact, Mr. Dacre. As

Sir Robert says, his daughter left here on Friday evening last, and she is due back again some time to-night. It was just a week-end visit. Surely it is some case of mistaken identity!"

"I wish to heaven it was," Dacre muttered fervently. "Unfortunately, it is only too true. Have you not read the morning papers, gentlemen?"

Dupont gave a little smothered cry.

His hand raised itself to his forehead.

He stared at Dacre with wild eyes.

"My God—" he commenced.

But the baronet only looked at both men in a dazed manner.

"No, I haven't glanced at the papers yet," he replied. "What has happened, Dacre? Tell me like a man. Don't prolong the agony in this fashion."

The expert handed him a copy of the London *Sentinel*.

Sir Robert put on his glasses with slow precision.

He read the account of the second airplane tragedy.

"That girl is your daughter!" Dacre said in a sad voice.

Sir Robert Anderson rose slowly to his feet.

Both his hands trembled.

A terrible greyness overspread his face.

"But how do you make that out?" he demanded. "My daughter has never gone up in an airplane. Not to my knowledge at least. I tell you she is with her cousin at Portland. Why do you keep on saying it is my daughter? Tell me the truth. What have you found? You are keeping something back!"

Dacre nodded.

"Yes, I discovered one pointer to identity," he answered, "and it was all I needed. I refer, Sir Robert, to the shoes worn by the girl in that airplane. They were only recently purchased from Marchland & Co., 17 Upper Brook Street, Weymouth. The size was 3½—an exceptionally small shoe—and both insteps had to be altered considerably. To make a long description short, the shoes had to be specially ordered for your daughter, and they were sent on to this hotel last Thursday night. The assistant described the purchaser to me with great accuracy, and that description is identical with the murdered girl. It is for you to confirm the dreadful tidings for yourself. May I offer my heartfelt sympathy, and my assurance that the murderer will yet be caught."

But the stricken baronet was not listening.

It is doubtful if he heard the last words.

He swayed like a drunken man and fell heavily on the floor.

CHAPTER XV

"FOLLOW MY LEADER"

BEFORE LUNCH, a message came through from Chief Constable Muir.

Dacre rushed to the telephone.

"Important news from Inspector Murray!" the Chief telephoned. "An airplane has landed at Mountdale, Mr. Dacre. It must be a new machine ordered by Major Frank Hardy. The plane came down inside the Mountdale grounds, and Hardy is giving it a thorough inspection. He may go off in it at any moment. What are your instructions?"

Dacre smiled.

He was always tickled to death by the panic of a Chief Constable.

"Well, if he goes off, give him my kind regards," Dacre said cynically. "But do not forget to keep him under observation, Chief, and ask Murray to report the next move without delay. I have not taken out an insurance policy on Hardy, but I am rather interested in his welfare. Also drop a word in the ear of Holmes. Tell him to keep off the drink and have his plane in readiness, and if Hardy is so mean as to go off without bidding us goodbye, tell Holmes to go up after him, and wish him God-speed. But tell him not to trail Hardy in too obvious a manner. I want information, not a capture. Do you understand, my dear Muir?"

"Quite, Mr. Dacre. Anything else?"

"Yes, I am going to have that inquest postponed. It would depress me terribly just now, so you must see the Coroner, and make the necessary application. You know, of course, that the second victim has been identified. I see it was in the noon edition of the local paper. Well, I cannot promise any fireworks, but there may be a chance of aircraft developments. They tell me Sir Robert Anderson went over to inspect the body. Poor old chap, I surmise he was in a bad state. He is nearly broken-hearted with grief."

"Yes, that girl was the light of his eye," the Chief Constable affirmed. "I never saw a man so fearfully upset, Mr. Dacre. Mr. Dupont brought him along in his private car, and when the baronet saw it was his only daughter, and witnessed the ghastly mutilation by the murderer's knife, heavens, I thought the shock was going to be too much for him. As it was, we had to carry him into another room, and that little nip of brandy from Gutteridge came in handy. Sir Robert collapsed in our hands, then cried for an hour like a child. I never want to see anything like that again. I fear he won't get over this business."

"Am afraid not," Dacre affirmed sympathetically. "He was certainly the picture of despair this morning, and he fell in a dead faint. I think his heart must be affected, so if a stroke comes, it is going to mean the end. Well, Muir, I am exceedingly obliged for ringing me up. I am just completing some important work in Weymouth, but do not forget to ring me up if there is anything fresh to report."

Dacre returned to the smokeroom, and found a cable awaiting him from Paris. It was a reply to the communication he had sent, and the contents gave him food for thought. He put that cablegram in his pocket, lit a cheroot, and flung himself in an armchair.

He reflected for an instant on M. Cambon. The erratic Frenchman had left the hotel before breakfast, sending Dacre just the briefest message he was going to London, but promising to get back again in a few hours. He had reserved his room at the hotel, taken no luggage, and so apparently it was just a rush visit to Town. That was the impression the *Sûreté* member created.

Yet Dacre shrugged his shoulders!

M. Cambon was an odd fish.

But was it a sign of genius or lunacy?

"Well, Big B., are you still dreaming about me? I suppose you thought I had gone for good, leaving Scotland Yard to pay my hotel bill? No, I don't do things like that!"

Dacre wheeled round to meet the radiant vision of Lena Somerton. He would never forget her loveliness at that moment. It was terrible to think that temptation in the form of such beauty existed. It also amazed him to realise that this girl, so far, had escaped. Why, she would have graced the table of any duke!

She had just returned from Portland, where he had sent her on a special mission.

"Good egg!" he exclaimed. "Glad to see you, Lena. You have just got back in time for lunch. But come and sit down a moment. I am just as ravenous as you are, but I am trying to control my impatience. I have it on good authority that a special chicken is being roasted in my honour, which means I am going to add a bottle of real French wine. But tell me what happened at Portland? What is the cousin's version of the affair? How was she affected by the murder of Louise Anderson? She knew nothing about the airplane, of course!"

"Heavens, how you talk," Lena said breathlessly. "Give me a cigarette, and I will love you for ever and a day!"

Dacre complied with the request.

She slipped into the nearest chair.

Her blue eyes were a trifle tired.

"Well, get on with it," he said peremptorily. "Who did you see in Portland?"

"I saw the cousin," Lena murmured softly. "Her full name is Lydia Montrose Campbell, and she lives with her parents in a villa close to the mainland. It is rather a big house, for they are notable people socially, and Louise paid them a visit twice a year. When I arrived, Miss Campbell heard the news an hour previously, and she had partly recovered from the shock. But she was in a terrible state of distress, and there was little information to be gained. Louise left Portland first thing on Sunday morning, merely hinting she had an appointment with a friend in Weymouth, but promising to return the following week-end. Her cousin accepted that promise in good faith, and that is all she knew about it,"

"No hint of a mystery-woman this time?"

"None whatever."

"And an airplane was never mentioned?"

"Louise never manifested any interest in flying. That is, no special interest, but like other girls of her age, she promised herself a flight one day. As for air-pilots, Miss Campbell is confident on that point. Neither she nor her cousin were acquainted with airmen. That means, my dear Dacre, so far as the Campbells are concerned, this second murder is an impenetrable mystery."

The expert gave a comprehensive nod.

"I had an idea nothing would materialise," he said quietly. "Not from the direction of Portland at least. Well, better come along and have some lunch. If you want to hear some exciting news, I have just had a 'phone message to say that Hardy has presented himself with a new plane, and may fly off in it at any moment. Now isn't that most impolite? But I have sent a special message to that rascal Holmes, with instructions to watch Hardy with the eyes of an eagle, and to make a special report about his movements. I believe Holmes won't let me down."

Lena leaned across the table.

They had just moved into the luncheon-room.

Only a few diners had as yet arrived.

"You think there may be some sudden development?"

"Yes," he said guardedly, "I rather imagine there will be a thunderstorm! But meanwhile there is no reason why we should starve. Waiter, I want your earnest attention for a few seconds. You may not believe it, but this luncheon is really a matter of life and death, for those who eat to-day may die to-morrow, and the two people you see before you are on the point of starvation. Now the hand holding the menu card is shaking visibly. Does that mean, my dear fellow, that you cannot recommend a single item with confidence, or does it mean the chicken has neither been caught nor killed?" He broke off to consider the suggestions on the card, and Lena watched him with smiling lips.

She leaned across when the waiter had gone.

"Do you know that Trevor Holmes rang me up?" she asked.

"I did not," Dacre answered promptly. "What the devil does he want? He can't borrow any money, and he knows I am employing you as confidential secretary—or so you think at least—so what is worrying him to-day? That young man, I fear, wants cooling medicine. He has smashed one Government plane already, and now he wants to flirt with you. Is that it?"

"Well, something to that effect," Lena replied with a wicked grin. "He thinks I am wasting my time in Weymouth—"

"Oh he does, does he?"

"And he suggests I go with him for a flip in that new plane. He is perfectly certain you could not have any objection."

The Yard man swore under his breath.

Lena wished he had said it aloud.

What was the good of cursing *sotto voce*?

"Well, it is the most asinine blunder Holmes has made," Dacre retorted. "I have given him special instructions about that plane, and by the lord Harry, if he disobeys them he is going to find himself in the soup. If he wants to make you a proposal of marriage, young lady, he had better come and consult me about it. I am acting as your legal and lawful guardian at the moment, and as this case is approaching an anticlimax, you had better stick to me like a limpet if you want a stupendous scoop for your paper."

Lena leaned back and laughed.

"You are under the spell of the green eye," she groaned. "You simply won't let me out of your sight. You are growing morbid with jealousy, Big Boy!"

Dacre regarded her sternly.

"Look here, there is one thing you must not do," he said gravely. "I have no objection to you messing about with

Holmes when it is convenient, but you must on no account go near Mountdale. Perhaps I am harbouring a truly unjust suspicion—which is not a habit of mine, by the way—but I did not relish the way Hardy glanced at you yesterday, so I do not want you to get into any trouble. That is the mildest way of putting it—"

The lovely face blanched a trifle.

"You really think that Hardy—"

"My dear young lady-journalist, I am not going to embark on any definite statement. I merely remark that the owner of Mountdale is a very interesting personage, and if you chance to meet him about Weymouth or elsewhere, I give you a solemn warning that you must not go near his place or enter his airplane. If you understand plain English, you cannot fail to interpret those words! But if you do insist on disregarding my advice, it will be at your own peril."

Lena pushed aside the soup plate.

"Very well, Mr. Cave-Man, I am listening," she beamed, "but that is not to say I am taking your advice. I promise to give it my earnest and careful consideration. Remember, please, that I have to consider the interests of my paper first, and if it occurs to me that I can pull off a scoop for the *Sentinel*, either by interviewing Hardy at Mountdale or going up in his new machine, I may forget all about your warning and think only of my duty. I am a free-lance first and a desperate little flirt afterwards!"

Dacre muttered something under his breath afresh.

It had a distinct reference to some foreign country.

Lena gave an instinctive shudder.

"There are some people who ought to be spanked and put to bed," he said severely. "You are one of them!"

"Will you do the spanking?"

"That all depends—"

As the luncheon proceeded, Dacre found himself gazing into those Mediterranean blue eyes. He wondered why they held such a magnetic influence! Was he merely studying the girl from a detached angle, or did it mean he was becoming interested in her as a human being? Strangely enough, his hatred of the opposite sex seemed an impersonal thing. He felt that one decent girl might exist in the whole crowd, but the only fault with Lena Somerton was her incurable pig-headedness! But that might not be a fault! Perhaps it was one of the new virtues?

"When are you going to make an arrest?"

"What do you mean?" he counter-asked.

"When are you going to arrest Major Frank Hardy for the murder of those two girls?"

"Who told you Major Frank Hardy murdered those two girls?"

Lena stared at him blankly.

This man always surprised her.

Was that why he was so attractive?

"No one, but what object had he in disguising himself as a woman?"

Dacre lit a cigarette with his coffee.

"My dear girl," he protested, "why should I arrest a man on a capital charge simply because he commits an act of folly? What judge or jury would convict Hardy on such slender evidence? Have I not pointed out that we want concrete proof of guilt, and even assuming that Hardy is the monster of the skies—I have never conceded that he was, remember—you forget that he has burnt his plane. He has destroyed all tangible evidence for a Criminal Court."

"So you are waiting to catch him red-handed?"

Dacre shrugged his shoulders.

"I never answer a question of that kind."

"But what about the hand-bag, the handkerchief, and the powder-puff?"

"Sufficient for you to know that they did not belong to Louise Anderson. No, I have verified that point already. The baronet has also confirmed it. So has the maid who attended his daughter when she was alive."

Lena looked far into space.

What kind of a mystery-man was the owner of Mountdale?

Should she slip over and interview him?

"And those other particulars he gave you about France?"

The dark eyes glowed.

"Ah, that is entirely a different question?" he reminded her.

Lena gave a little gasp.

"You infer they were not correct, that he was only bluffing you about the Parisienne—?"

"I infer nothing," was the steady answer. "But I prefer to keep my lips sealed for the present. All the subtleties of your journalistic profession will not force me to say a word . . . Now what the blazes does this waiter want?"

It was another urgent call to the telephone.

This time it was Inspector Frank Murray.

His voice contained a ring of excitement.

"Some special news, Mr. Dacre!" he exclaimed. "Major Hardy has just left Mountdale in his new airplane. Acting on instructions, Captain Holmes entered his machine and went after him."

"What direction have they gone, Murray?"

"That is just the funny part," replied the Inspector. "At first it looked as if Hardy was making for the Channel, but immediately he perceived another machine was following him, he changed his programme and made for Weymouth. Now he has returned in the direction of Cottingdale, with Captain Holmes keeping him steadily trailed, and both machines are performing all kinds of antics. It is almost laughable. Hardy has looped for the past five or ten minutes, then climbed as far as fourteen thousand feet, hoping to get the other machine off his track, or trying to disappear behind the clouds, but there happens to be almost a cloudless sky, and Holmes is playing with him like a cat. It looks as if Hardy realised the game was up. He is now heading back for home!"

Dacre permitted himself a grin.

"An amusing comedy, eh? Well, you are all having value for your money to-day, Murray. I am glad Holmes is sticking to him. He has received his definite instructions in the matter, and I hardly think he will let Hardy go. Let us hope there will be no sensational accident."

"Thought it best to notify you, Mr. Dacre."

"Where are you speaking from?"

"A public call-office on the Cottingdale road—about a hundred yards past the station. I can see both planes at the moment. Hardy has turned again in the direction of the Channel, but Holmes is following him like a bloodhound. Ah, there they go again. They have started another fantastic looping business. Can't make it out at all. What is the game, I wonder?"

Dacre sent a laugh along the wire.

"I think it is all pretty obvious," he said, gaily. "Hardy is trying to throw the other plane off the scent. Very well, I will get the car out and see the fun, Murray. You can expect me along in a few minutes!"

Lena was tremendously thrilled by that ride.

Dacre, of course, was a demon driver, and that afternoon he simply flew along the Weymouth road.

When the car pulled up alongside Cottingdale Police Station, they found a little crowd had collected. Prominent amongst them were Chief Constable Muir and P.C. Gutteridge. The latter had armed himself with a huge pair of opera-glasses! They were all gazing up to the sky, and no wonder! Two planes were performing the weirdest and funniest convolutions! Looping, spinning, stalling, then a mad dash through space with the other machine on its tail! What did it mean?

Chief Constable Muir came over at once.

"I can't make it out, Mr. Dacre," he gasped. "What are they playing at? That white plane belongs to Captain Trevor Holmes—it was the one that came yesterday afternoon—and the black plane is being controlled by Major Hardy. Both of them, beyond a doubt, are experienced pilots, but all that stunting in the air seems a trifle mysterious. What is the big idea behind it all? Is Holmes just playing a game of some kind?"

Dacre watched for a few seconds in silence.

Then he doubled up laughing.

His eyes sparkled with merriment.

"It amounts to nothing more than that," he said carelessly. "Hardy is trying to wear out Holmes by darting all over the show, but Holmes can play the same game till sundown. We have often put up a show of that kind at Northolt. It is called 'Follow my Leader,' and is most interesting until the crash comes. There is always a crash at the end, you know."

P.C. Gutteridge ventured on a profound remark.

"I don't mind tricks of that kind," he said in an impressive whisper. "But what I objects to see, Mr. Dacre, is the circus business! You know what I mean—what I saw on Saturday afternoon. A machine circling round seventeen times until it makes you giddy, and then a human body being flung overboard to the earth. Ugh, I haven't slept a wink since."

Dacre flashed him a glance of commiseration.

"Still, you have the brandy bottle," he reminded him. "But don't give me the creeps, my dear Gutteridge. I saw that circus business myself yesterday morning, and once in a lifetime is quite sufficient . . . Ah, look, Hardy is making for Mountdale with a vengeance, and there goes Holmes at his heels. They are both coming down inside the Mountdale grounds. Let's see if we can get some rational explanation."

He shot the car forward, and in a few seconds was speeding up the Mountdale drive.

He was just in time to witness the two planes come to earth. Both made a perfect landing, and then Hardy jumped from his machine like some infuriated beast of the jungle.

There was a white foam at his mouth.

His teeth clenched in some wild rage.

His eyes stared in their sockets.

"What the blazes do you mean?" he shouted at the advancing Holmes. "What the hell did you want by keeping on my tail? Does it mean, Holmes, that you are nothing but a confounded police spy, a dirty rat sent out by Scotland Yard, that your job is to dog my footsteps from morn till night?"

Holmes calmly lit a cigarette.

"Nothing of the kind, my dear fellow," he answered placidly. "I have just heard you had bought a new bus, Hardy, and as the Government has favoured me with one as well, I thought you might enjoy a little game called 'Follow my Leader.' If you have failed to appreciate the joke, there is really no need to burst a blood-vessel. Have a cigarette and be damned to you!"

CHAPTER XVI

EXCHANGE IS NO ROBBERY!

IT WAS Lena who poured oil on the waters. She jumped from the car with a light laugh.

Manifestly she was pleased to see Trevor Holmes.

"So you two have been behaving like a pair of butterflies," she announced. "Chasing each other about the heavens as if you were both demented. Perhaps both of them are insane, Dacre! Do you think we should have them examined?"

"It certainly looked as if you were both qualifying for asylum tickets," Dacre declared, "but I must say I enjoyed the little exhibition of aerobatics. Now if you would both undertake to repeat that performance at a Weymouth Air Carnival, there would be no need to lift a collection for the local hospital."

Holmes gave another hearty laugh.

He was staring at Dacre in significant fashion.

It was plainly a warning that Hardy had to be watched.

"I am ready to give an air circus any day you name, Dacre," he responded genially, "but to make the thing absolutely realistic, I suggest that Hardy gives us another thrilling parachute descent. Good-afternoon, Miss Somerton, I see you have only recognised my existence by the merest nod, but I presume you entertain towards me a slight measure of friendliness?"

"Very slight," Lena sighed. Then she turned to Hardy. "I see you have bought a lovely little two-seater Avro, Major. Wouldn't I just love to have a flip in it."

Hardy changed his mood to the new comers.

He waved his hand genially to the Scotland Yard man.

Lena he welcomed with a brilliant smile.

"My dear young lady," he replied, "I shall be charmed any day and any hour to give you a trip in that machine. Come along now, if you like, and perhaps Captain Holmes will not worry me any more with his silly air-games! What do you say, Dacre? Has Miss Somerton your permission to accompany me on a short flight? I promise to bring her back inside the hour."

Lena saw that it was a difficult question.

She gave a little roguish smile.

Was Dacre cornered?

"I think there is some misunderstanding," the expert said easily. "Miss Somerton has already secured her flying ticket, Hardy, and you could not please her better than allow her to handle that machine. Let her do a few stunts, and if she comes to earth with a horrible bump, then we will both collect the insurance money."

Hardy gave an acclamation of pleasure.

He never dreamt the girl could handle a joy-stick.

His interest in her increased. "Why, of course," he assented readily.

"I don't mind in the least. Let us see what you can do in the air, Miss Somerton, but for heaven's sake don't give us any sensational stunts. Holmes, stand by to give that prop. a turn. Now then, young lady, up you go and the best of luck!"

Lena clapped her hands in great glee.

She ran to the new Avro with a little cry of delight.

Not for months had she a chance of a flip!

"Now for the love of Mike," Holmes shouted, with one hand on the propeller, "don't forget that I am afflicted with cardiac trouble. And if you are not back inside twenty minutes, then I will go up after you and drag you down."

Lena climbed into the cockpit.

She liked the look of this dainty Avro.

Somehow she could not associate it with Hardy!

"I wish I had money to buy this machine," she exclaimed rapturously, examining the interior of the cockpit with manifest delight. "But why were the wings painted black, Major

Hardy? That is the only thing depressing about it. Perhaps you wanted it to represent something dark and mysterious! How positively thrilling. Are you ready, Holmes?"

"At your service, my lady," that individual called out.

"Contact!"

In a few seconds the dainty plane glided forward along the grass, rose in a beautiful glide to the clear sky, and then soared gracefully over the top of Mountdale. It was a splendid "take-off," and even Holmes clapped his hands involuntarily.

The three men watched the girl-flier!

She was ascending with effortless ease.

The Avro climbed to something like six thousand feet!

"By Jove, she can fly!" Hardy exclaimed with genuine admiration. "Look at that magnificent turn, Dacre! Ah, a loop! Good girl! Bravo. Well done, well done!" He was watching the aerobatics of the Avro with the enthusiasm of a schoolboy, and the other two men were as keenly interested. Lena was an accomplished lady pilot. There was no doubt on that point. But was she not overdoing it?

Holmes watched quietly.

He was tickled to death at some of the convolutions.

He knew the girl was just playing a few monkey tricks.

"I wish she would exercise more commonsense!" Dacre said solemnly. "I don't wish to be convinced she can loop. She has demonstrated that once already, but that never-ending series is rather a strain on the nerves. I often wonder if a girl can stand that looping as much as a man! There—by God, I thought that was a nose-dive! The little fool! Why does she behave in that mad fashion! Ah, a spiral spin for a change. Good for you, Lena Somerton! I wish we could have you photographed for the *Sentinel*. The Editor would give you promotion right away. Heavens, did you see that, Holmes? She brought the machine almost over our heads! Now why the blazes does she go in for that low flying! It always means a crash!"

Holmes gave a quiet chuckle.

He was watching the flight with the keen eyes of a critic.

The girl intrigued him vastly.

"Don't worry," he counselled. "That little piece of femininity knows how to take care of herself. She can handle that joy-stick to perfection. But I must warn her to shut off that engine a little faster. She turns the nose of the machine too far down before—Phew, that was a close shave. You are right, Dacre. I wish she would exercise a little more common-sense!" The Avro had just performed an ugly-looking somersault, and the plane seemed to quiver after the performance.

Major Hardy was unperturbed.

"The machine will stand it all right," he observed. "I only wish I had a girl of that age to give us such a fine exhibition. Never dreamt she was an efficient air-pilot, Dacre. 'Pon my soul, she ought to go in for the flying business properly. She would make her fortune in the near future. Do you think—"

He paused.

All three held their breath.

Was it going to be tragedy?

The Avro dashed downward in a terrific dive, with the engine roaring like an infuriated monster, then, just before the lowest point of the earth could be reached, it flattened out and mounted again to the clear, calm sky! It was the most reckless dive either of those men had witnessed. They looked at each other in silence. Death had been missed by inches.

"By God, a splendid nerve!" Dacre muttered. "But we had better get her down, Holmes. I fear she is only stunting for our amusement, and we don't want the girl to crash, do we? Look what she is doing now! Flying upside down, by the lord Harry! Say, Hardy, you never gave us that stunt, did you? Now there is a picture for you, but if she breaks her silly little neck, she will only have herself to blame."

Holmes was doubled up laughing.

He thought it the finest spectacle for ages.

Why, it even beat cock-fighting.

"Ah, she has waved her handkerchief," he muttered. "She is going off for a real flight. No chance of seeing that girl again before Christmas, Dacre. She has either gone to Australia or the other end of the earth."

It was true.

The Avro was soaring away into space.

It was travelling fast in the direction of the Channel.

"Well, let us have a look at this new plane of yours, Holmes!" It was the Yard man who made the suggestion, and all three strolled to the machine with the white wings. It was the latest type of Bristol Fighter, with a new and wonderfully-designed engine, and the three men examined it from all angles.

"She flies beautifully," Holmes remarked, with an appreciative smile. "And the engine hums as musically as a golden-throated canary. A perfect even stroke from beginning to end. Nothing of the tin-Lizzie about this, I assure you. Wish to heaven they would allocate it to me definitely, but I expect it has been handed out as an emergency ration."

"Do you mind if I give it a test flight?" Major Hardy asked with a delightfully-innocent air. His request seemed a perfectly logical one. How would the Yard man deal with it? Holmes threw Dacre a rather comical glance.

But Dacre was seldom caught napping.

His features remained inscrutable.

Only the faintest smile appeared at the corner of his mouth.

"Go right ahead," he said genially. "Have a buzz round in it, Hardy, and if you don't mind I will occupy the back seat." He added the last sentence with the utmost *sang-froid*, and Holmes made a tremendous effort to keep from choking! He wanted to shriek with laughing. How the clever Major was outwitted!

But wait!

Hardy had still a card to play.

He merely shrugged his shoulders.

"No," he said suddenly, "that would be too discourteous on my part. After all, you two men are my guests. You have come to Mountdale to be entertained, and I must do my part of it. You have never been inside my place, Holmes? Come along and let me show you a few of the treasures! And you also, Dacre. I have a surprise in store for you. You only saw the huge library when you paid your last visit. I have never shown you my special art gallery. I think more of my pictures than anything else on earth. Come!"

Dacre and Hardy exchanged another significant glance.

The girl-journalist had disappeared into the empyrean.

There was nothing for it but to fall in with the suggestion.

"Well, I'm dashed!" Holmes exclaimed, as he mounted the white terrace steps and surveyed the vast mansion belonging to Hardy. "Never thought you had such a magnificent place, my old dear! One of these days I must take a run over that golf-course! And what lovely flower-beds! Gee, Hardy, you must be a millionaire"

"Ah, that is a State secret," Hardy exclaimed with a mysterious smile. "Put me down for the present as a financier! Nothing more or less. Here, come into the library a second! What about a cocktail, Holmes? I can offer you something specially new in that line. One moment and I will give the butler explicit instructions."

That was the only blunder Dacre made.

He dared to rely on the good faith of his host.

He never dreamt it was a piece of capital bluff.

"Well, what do you think of this magnificent library?" Holmes asked, glancing round the room with unstinted admiration. "Gee, old-timer, Hardy has been accumulating books for the last two centuries! Did you ever see such a collection in your life. You don't mean to say he is a philosopher as well! How the devil does he get time to read all these!"

Dacre gave a contemptuous smile.

"These books are never read," he said quietly. "Major Hardy is nothing but a faddist in some respects. He is a collector of books just as, I presume, he is a collector of pictures. I am anxious to see his art-gallery. That will be a real test. I have never put him down as a connoisseur in that respect. One can buy even a certain number of good books, but one often becomes a clown when purchasing so-called Rembrandts! Now when are these cocktails going to put in an appearance?"

It was the first note of suspicion that entered Dacre's voice, and the moment it left his lips he knew he was too late.

Holmes dashed to the window.

Dacre never moved.

He realised with a groan that he had been duped.

"By God, he's off!" Holmes exclaimed with an oath. "Lord, we were fools, Dacre, to let him steal a march on us. And in my plane, too! What an infernal cheek!"

The butler arrived with the cocktails.

"Drink them yourself," Dacre said calmly. "We are going outside, my friend, to inspect your chicken-house!"

The two friends descended the white steps together.

Holmes was swearing like a trooper.

Dacre wore that inscrutable smile.

"And look at the direction he has taken?" Holmes exclaimed, pointing to the rapidly-disappearing Bristol Fighter. "He is making for the Channel also! What the devil does it mean, Dacre? Why is he trying to escape? You don't really think he is the murderer, do you? If so, why did you allow him to slip through your hands in that fashion?"

Dacre shrugged his shoulders.

Then he proffered his cigarette-case.

Both men lit up.

"I have nothing against Hardy in the shape of concerted evidence," he said simply, "but I was keeping him under observation for a purpose. As it is, I am not going to excite myself by what has happened. I know exactly where he has gone, and why he has undertook the mission; and perhaps in the end Fate will play right into my hands. Don't worry, Holmes. When the time comes for me to arrest my man—and I am not saying it is Major Hardy, remember—I shall know exactly where to find him."

The young Air Force officer regarded his companion with awe.

Dacre was a greater enigma than ever.

There was something wonderfully attractive about him.

"Then Hardy is not the man you want?" he queried.

Dacre laughed as they crossed the lawn.

"Don't ask silly questions," he replied. "Here is that black Avro returning. Thank heaven, the girl is still safe. She has not exceeded her twenty minutes after all. Look, she has shut off the engine. What a lovely descent!"

Yes, it was a perfect landing, and when Lena jumped lightly from the cockpit of the machine, Dacre had no need to regret he missed seeing the art-gallery. Lena Somerton was a picture of real loveliness. In a word, she was like an angel descended from the clouds, but he would not permit himself to use such metaphor in speech!

"Well," she exclaimed with a wonderful laugh, "what are you two babes looking so glum about! I have just been having the time of my life in that adorable Avro, and now I come back to find you almost in tears. Where is Hardy? And good heavens, where is your machine, Holmes?"

She stared round the deserted field.

No Bristol Fighter and no suspected murderer!

Something had gone wrong!

"Hardy played an ace when poor Dacre was woolgathering!" Holmes explained in a sepulchral voice. "We were led into a kind of ambush. Pushed into the library, offered cocktails that might have been poisoned, and then given the glorious sight of Hardy disappearing in the clouds. I could kick myself for an hour, and I know Dacre wants to commit suicide."

Lena ran forward to the expert.

Her features were aghast with astonishment.

Dacre confronted her with a smile.

"Is this true?" she asked breathlessly. "Have you allowed that dreadful man to escape? Dacre, you could never have been such a fool!"

The Yard expert only grinned.

"Major Hardy had an important appointment in Paris," he explained, "and he found it impossible to say good-bye! But I have reserved for myself the last trick. That perhaps will prove the most potential of all. Come along, he has left us the police-car at least. Let us get back to Weymouth. You come along as well, Holmes. Perhaps you will find another plane washed up by the waves!"

They entered the police-car in a stern silence.

Holmes flung himself in the back seat and yawned.

Lena took her place at the wheel.

"According to the law of compensation," she murmured in a wicked voice, "we ought to set fire to that hideous black plane. Why should we make him a present of two machines?"

Holmes jumped out of the car like a shot.

"By God, you're right!" he exclaimed. "Drive on back to Weymouth, Dacre! I am going to adopt this Avro in case of another emergency. Exchange is no robbery!"

Dacre gave a nod of approval.

"I was just going to make the suggestion," he said with a strange smile.

CHAPTER XVII

A KISS!

THE POLICE-CAR dashed down the drive. It passed through the open Mountdale gates.

Then it pulled up on the country road.

"Why are you looking so perplexed?" Dacre addressed the query to Inspector Frank Murray, who was still keeping observation on the estate.

Murray gave a sharp salute.

"I beg your pardon, Mr. Dacre," he answered, "but I was just in a bit of a quandary. I had no idea what was going on up at Mountdale, and when I saw the black plane go off in the direction of the Channel, I wondered if you were allowing Hardy to get away. Then I was bewildered when the Avro machine returned to Mountdale, and I wondered who could have been inside it. Now the Bristol Fighter has gone off in the direction of the Channel, and I am more astonished than ever. Perhaps you will explain, sir!"

Dacre gave a disarming smile.

"Murray," he replied, "I owe you an apology. I should have brought you along to Hardy's place, and then you would have seen everything for yourself. As a matter of fact, there has been a slight blunder on my part, but everything will turn out for the best. If you want to know the truth, Hardy went off just now in that Bristol Fighter—"

"Alone?"

"Yes, alone," Dacre affirmed. "He outwitted us rather cleverly. When you saw the Avro go up a second time, it was just a little demonstration of stunt-flying by Miss Somerton—ahem, the young lady at the wheel—and when she went off for a flight, Major Hardy invited us into his house with some pretence of showing his art-gallery. He first led us into the library, after which he went away to order some special cocktails, and I was foolish enough not to keep my eyes open. You can picture the rest for yourself. When our backs were turned, he darted like a shot across the lawn, climbed into that Bristol Fighter, and, with the aid of the efficient self-starting apparatus, got away like a flash of lightning."

Murray gave a hollow groan.

"And what happened to the Avro?" he questioned.

"Captain Trevor Holmes has commandeered that for the present," Dacre answered. "I expect he will fly it back to the field near the police station . . . No, by George, look where he is going!"

They all stared breathlessly into the sky.

Holmes had taken off splendidly, and was travelling fast in the direction of the Channel!

Was it true?

Was he making a desperate effort to overtake Hardy?

It looked mighty like it.

"Say, that's great!" Lena said in a burst of admiration. "He has gone after your suspect, Dacre, and I believe he will catch him. Remember, he has got a Bristol bus, with one of the new model Jupiter engines, and at the rate he is going, no Avro could possibly keep ahead of him. He will do it. Look, he has disappeared into space already. He's flying high too. My word, but Hardy is in for a surprise!"

Dacre gave a little chuckle.

"That's mighty fine of Holmes," he observed. "No idea he had it in him. That shows what can be done by acting on your own initiative. Well, I think you are right, young lady. I believe the Bristol Fighter is going to reach the French coast first, or at least he is bound to trail Hardy to his landing-place. After that the rest will be easy. Come along, we had better get back to Weymouth. Meanwhile, Murray, do not relax your vigilance on Mountdale. Post special men on duty, have them relieved at intervals, and make your report to me in the usual fashion. You know where to find me at Claridge's."

"Very good, Mr. Dacre." The Inspector touched his cap again, and Lena sent the police-car on a fast spin down the road. She would not admit it to herself, but she was secretly pleased at her flip in the Avro machine, and more thrilled than ever to realise that Dacre was again by her side. Why did the presence of this man send the blood tingling through her veins?

"Are both your parents alive?" he asked irrelevantly.

Lena sat up with a start.

"Of course," she answered. "They are both living in the duckiest little house at South Kensington. Why do you manifest concern over my relatives? Are you thinking of sending me back to them?"

Dacre grinned.

"It might not be the worst plan," he temporised. "Especially if you go performing mad, fantastic freaks in an airplane. Do you know you went perilously near being killed this afternoon? Another inch nearer the ground and that machine would have earthed itself like a pancake, but you would never have known about it. The engine would have caught fire at once, and we would have been trying to put out a flaming furnace! Gad, you did give me an unholy shiver!"

Lena looked at him steadily.

The crimson entered both her cheeks.

She was particularly entrancing at that moment.

"Perhaps that is why I acted so foolishly," she ventured. "Maybe I wanted to find out if you were interested in my unworthy self? You see, I thought you hated me so terribly, and I fancied it would be a good idea to find out if it was really true. Is it?"

Dacre kept his eyes averted.

He was afraid to glance into that lovely face.

He knew it was a weak instant.

"Don't be absurd," he answered. "And for heavens' sake don't think you've got hold of a joy-stick! That happens to be the driving-wheel of this car, and if you don't keep to the right side of the road, there is going to be a stupendous calamity. Hate you? Of course I detest every member of your sex. I exclude only one woman from the list of my sex-enemies. That is my own mother—and she happens to be an angel."

Lena felt inclined to pinch him.

She loved teasing this man.

At times he had the temperament of a schoolboy.

"But you don't give me the chance of being an angel," she pouted. "Look how nice I might be to you, Dacre, if you only permitted yourself a little flirtation. Now I do look tempting, don't I? Won't you give me one little kiss? Just one!"

She meant it only in jest.

But the sequel proved terrific.

Dacre suddenly complied with her request.

And what a kiss! She would remember it all her life. For one heavenly instant he held her close in his arms, pressing her lips against his in a passionate contact, then he calmly lit a cigarette, and looked as if nothing had happened.

He realised it was his second blunder that day.

But the girl had distinctly asked for it.

And, after all, what is a kiss?

Yet Lena knew that it meant a great deal more indeed! It made her speechless for the remainder of the journey, although from time to time she gave shy little reproachful glances at the man who had kissed her. Yes, that kiss was something she would remember all through eternity!

She ran up to her own room the moment the hotel was reached.

It was a time for self-analysis.

What had happened?

Was she really in love with Dacre?

She thought for an instant of Trevor Holmes and his boyish, handsome face! There was something desperately winning about Holmes. He was so daring, vital, and alive! His laugh seemed to be the sweetest thing on earth, and yet—! Well, Dacre had got hold of her in some mysterious fashion. At first he had roused in her a strong sense of sex-antagonism, generated of course by his open declaration of hostility, and then that antagonism had slowly, gradually changed.

There was something magnetic about Dacre that gripped.

His dark eyes contained unfathomable depths.

The way he looked at her sometimes made her gasp!

And then she started thinking about him. Had he merely kissed her as a passive act of flirtation, just as she wished, merely to show that he was not afraid to comply with her request? That was a tantalising thought. If he only meant that, if there was nothing deeper than a passing kiss in a motor-car, then her hatred of him would know no bounds! There could be no punishment too great for him. And in revenge she would make him pay for that kiss!

For it had consumed her like new wine!

She knew it was different to any she had ever experienced.

Never would she forget that mad, tempestuous embrace!

Then the smile returned to her lips, and she spent the next half-hour making herself more attractive than ever. They would have tea together, and she would coax him to take her a walk through Weymouth. It was a glorious evening, and they would both want to forget the horror of the morning! A walk along the pier with the famous Scotland Yard expert. That seemed the most glorious programme her mind could conjure.

But when she went downstairs there was no sign of Dacre.

Instead she had a tremendous surprise.

The man waiting for her was Captain Trevor Holmes!

"What has happened, and where is Dacre?" she enquired in one breath, as he led her into the nearest tea-room. "And why have you returned to us so suddenly? Have you tracked Hardy to his lair, or did you lose sight of him in the clouds? You have never been to France and back in this time!"

Trevor gave a loud laugh.

"France?" he exclaimed. "Oh, do give me a chance, Lena. Why, it has just gone five o'clock! No, one of your guesses was correct. Hardy gave me the slip from the start. I never really caught sight of him after I left Cottingdale. That means, I suppose, that he flew towards the Channel for a blind, then got up into the clouds and turned inland somewhere. I have just seen Dacre and explained the whole matter. He has gone upstairs to have a few words with Sir Robert Anderson. Poor old man, I hear he has taken this second tragedy to heart!"

"No wonder!" Lena answered. "Louise was his only daughter. It was nice of Dacre to pay him another call. I think he is exceptionally human at times, don't you?"

The waiter brought the tea things.

Lena poured out the precious stuff!

She was watching Holmes with one eye.

"Look here," he said swiftly, "I want you to forget all about Dacre. Do you know why I am glad Hardy has got away? Well, for the time being at least? Just because it has given me the opportunity for a personal chat. Lena, I am going to ask you something terribly important. Will you marry me at the end of this month?"

"Good heavens!"

Lena placed the teapot down and stared.

Holmes had not known her twenty-four hours!

And he had just proposed marriage!

"I know it's a bit sudden-like," he continued boyishly, "but I was taught at Cambridge never to neglect a golden opportunity, and—!"

Lena burst out laughing.

She was tickled to death.

This was more amazing than growing an orchid in a night.

"You don't mean to say you are in earnest?" she giggled.

"Of course I am! Say the answer is in the affirmative, and I will buy the ring to-morrow. A special licence will do the trick, and then I can obtain ten days' official leave. We can borrow that Avro for the honeymoon, Lena, and hey presto—it will mean Paris, the French Riviera, and on to Switzerland! Is it a bargain? Say, little girl, you are not going to turn me down?"

Lena poured him out a second cup of tea.

"You big, silly chump," she said laughing. "Of course, I am going to turn you down! Why stupid, I never thought you were so insane as all that. Besides, you have never asked me if there was anyone else?"

Holmes stared at her incredulously.

His face seemed quite grave.

He was really hurt over it.

"But I felt perfectly certain on that point," he gasped. "You don't mean to say you are going to get hitched up with your editor, or some grisly old fossil like that?"

Lena nearly shrieked.

Instead she helped herself to marmalade.

She also assisted herself again to the teapot.

"Oh heavens, but you'll be the death of me!" she exclaimed. "Listen, Trevor Holmes, once upon a time a man kissed me! . . . I am not sure what he meant by that kiss. I am not sure what I meant when I allowed him to kiss me . . . Until the answer to those queries are discovered, I am going to postpone all ideas of matrimony. Now shut up fooling, for goodness sake, and concentrate on this meal."

Holmes leaned forward.

His handsome face smote the girl's heart.

He was terrifically good-looking!

"Who was the blighter that kissed you?" he demanded. "I know! . . . It was Dacre! . . . Yes, I guessed it first time! He has been fooling round you in that car. He is trying to flirt with you, but it is just a little game of his, and he means nothing by it. He thinks you rather a pretty London journalist, a girl who might give him a good time—"

"Stop!" . . . Lena's face was convulsed. Never had she looked so frightfully angry. The blue eyes were positively fierce. "Another word, Holmes, and I will forget myself. Don't ever express yourself in that manner again. Dacre is nothing to me—nothing whatever. Do you hear?"

Holmes was bewildered.

He half rose and made an apology.

Lena accepted it with a forced smile.

"My dear girl, I am stupendously sorry," he exclaimed. "I never thought you would go into such a paddy over a little thing like that. Why, I was only teasing! . . . Say, Lena, I have had to come along and make my report to Dacre, but now that's over, I am free for an hour or two. Will you come a stroll along the Weymouth pier and let us be friends again?"

The girl gave him her hand.

"Of course we are friends," she said gaily. "Where is the Avro, by the way?"

"I have berthed it in the same shed I used for the Bristol Fighter-quite close to Cottingdale Police Station—and P.C. Gutteridge is keeping a careful eye on it. Say the word, and we will have that walk?"

Lena rose to her feet.

"Do you mind if I bring a girl friend?" she asked.

Holmes paused in the act of lighting a cigarette.

It was a test moment but he conquered.

His mouth relaxed.

"Of course not!" he answered boyishly. "*Qui est la femme?*"

"A very humble little factory worker named Mary Brookes," Lena explained. "If you come out on the hotel terrace, I will tell you all about her. She and I are on the lookout for a mystery-woman, and perhaps tonight we are going to be lucky. You can come along and help."

They moved out on the terrace together.

Meanwhile Dacre was having tea upstairs with Sir Robert Anderson, the father of the murdered girl. It was just an act of special consideration on the detective's part, for he happened to realise that the baronet had received a stupendous blow, and perhaps he could cheer him up to some extent.

They were sitting in the financier's private suite.

Tea had just been served, and the pair were drinking it together.

Tears still rained down the baronet's cheek.

"I am making a fresh will," he said in a low voice. "You see, Dacre, I already feel my days on earth are numbered. Louise was the most precious thing I possessed, and now that she has gone—"

He broke down afresh.

The tea-cup shook in his hand.

Dacre took it from him and placed it on the small table.

"I have a good idea how you feel, Sir Robert," he said in a kind voice, "and I have come to make a very practical suggestion. You are right in saying that the blow is terrible, and how deeply you have been affected, but now is the time for you to get a tight hold on yourself. I mean this: you want to make a strong effort to distract your mind, because if you go on fretting over this business—"

"What do you suggest?" the baronet interrupted. "Leave England for a year? How would that do? Perhaps that might be one way out—"

"Something infinitely better than that!" Dacre suggested.

"What is it? Tell me what it is, Dacre? I am prepared to do practically anything you say. I like you, my boy, and I believe you are going to see that murder avenged. Now tell me, like a good fellow. How am I going to forget Louise?"

"Not forget her," Dacre corrected. "That is impossible. But you can bring comfort and practical help to another man who has received the same blow as yourself. I refer to poor old Robert Henderson, the bereaved father of the first victim! He is lonely and friendless, living at 3 Moorgate Street, Weymouth, and his daughter was murdered in the same fashion as your Louise—"

The baronet pushed the tea table aside.

He rose unsteadily to his feet.

But there was a different look about his stricken face.

"My God, you are right!" he said hoarsely. "Get hold of a taxi, Dacre. I will go there without delay. I know exactly what to say to that man—and he knows—what to say to me . . . We both need each other, and if I can help him financially—Here, reach me that stick!"

CHAPTER XVIII

CAUGHT!

CLARIDGE'S HOTEL that Monday evening at midnight.

The corridors were empty.

A profound stillness reigned throughout the building.

Then a door opened on the second landing, and a figure emerged. It was a tall woman in a dark green dress. She walked with quiet deliberation to the far end of the passage, with a tread that in itself was absolutely noiseless, looked over the stairs to make certain no one was about, and then approached Room 17 on that landing.

It was the bedroom booked by Lena Somerton of the *Sentinel*.

The woman turned the handle of the door.

It was a successful effort, for the door opened at once.

The room was in complete darkness, so the woman in the dark green dress stepped inside and closed the door gently behind her. She made no effort to switch on the electric light. Instead something flashed in her hand, and she moved stealthily towards the bed.

She was just about to spring like a tiger on that sleeping figure when a stern voice pierced the darkness.

"Stand exactly where you are!"

Then the light was flashed on with uncanny swiftness, and the woman in the dark green dress found herself looking down Malcolm Dacre's revolver.

The other figure sprang from the bed.

It was the wide-awake Inspector Frank Murray!

And he wore his official uniform.

"I beg your pardon," said the woman in the dark green dress, "but really it was quite an oversight. I must have made a mistake. I think I have entered the wrong room. But the lights in the corridor have been partly extinguished, and I suppose the mistake was natural!" Whilst speaking, she made a tremendous effort to hide what she held in her hand.

"Put that knife on the table!" Dacre commanded in the same stern voice. "Now, Murray, let us see how quick you can be with those bracelets . . . Ah, too late!" His warning proved correct, for no sooner had the woman placed the knife on the table than she slipped something into her mouth.

"Yes, you are too late," the woman said in a hoarse voice. "But allow me to congratulate you, Malcolm Dacre, on an exceedingly smart piece of work. I presume, you see, that the incriminating clue has been carefully secured, but at least I am going to evade the gallows. In four minutes I shall be dead. Quick, how did you work this problem out! I thought I had baffled you completely!"

The woman slipped down on the side of the bed.

Murray supported her shoulders with one hand.

The poison was doing its deadly work.

"You made a desperate mistake, M. Cambon, when you thought you could get away with that dual personality stunt!" The voice of Malcolm Dacre was cold and precise. "Indeed, to be perfectly candid, you made a whole series of blunders, and I could have arrested you many hours ago only I determined to catch you red-handed. As it is, I took Inspector Murray into my confidence, and staged this last act in the terrible drama. You walked into the trap—you, the most distinguished member of the French *Sûreté*. Man, I am horrified. What is that stuff you have taken? Is there no hope? Can nothing be done to save your life temporarily at least?"

The face on the bed was turning grey.

The lips twitched convulsively.

The end was very near.

"Nothing can be done," M. Cambon muttered. "You have proved yourself a genius, Dacre, and all that remains for me is death. Tell me how you got on my track!"

It was a dramatic moment.

Dacre took a chair and leaned across.

Murray still supported his dying prisoner.

"You never succeeded in disguising your voice," the Yard expert continued. "That meant, M. Cambon, that the personation of Major Frank Hardy was not quite a success. I admit your disguise as Hardy was very clever, but again your eyes betrayed you, and then you made the biggest blunder of your life!"

"What was that?"

The voice was very weak.

"You showed me that ivory cross on your watch-chain. That talisman proved your undoing. It confirmed my suspicions . . . You see, Cambon, I happen to be blessed with a singularly good memory. You forgot that seven years ago you showed me that same ivory cross at Ostend, and I knew there was no other talisman like it in the world."

"*Mon Dieu!*" the dying man muttered. "Go on. What else did you discover?"

"Your diary. You made the colossal mistake of making entries in your diary, and I took the first opportunity of inspecting your room at this hotel. The diary I found in your private despatch-box which you kept at the bottom of your trunk. I always read diaries, M. Cambon, and that chronicle of your double life would be quite sufficient for any jury. As it is, you have decided on this other way out—"

"And that is how you trapped me tonight?" The Frenchman's voice was gradually getting weaker.

"Yes," Dacre continued imperturbably, "I read the profound impression made on you by Miss Somerton, and you were so confident in your dual personality—or perhaps it was your sublime egotism—that you made that terrible entry concerning what would happen to-night at this hour. That enabled me to transfer the girl to another room, and arrange this ambush for yourself."

"When did you discover that diary?"

"This afternoon when you were flying to Paris and back! That was the second time I inspected the contents of your room, unknown to you of course! On the first occasion, the evidence of the diary eluded my grasp. But I did not take possession of it. That would have given the game away. Now about the cablegram you sent me from France to-day. It arrived safely before supper, but there was really no necessity for it. You see, M. Cambon, I had already cabled a friend in Paris, who informed me that the statements of Major Frank Hardy were a tissue of lies. The French railway syndicate knew nothing about him. Neither did the *Hotel Carillon* in the *Bois de Ventome*, and no plane belonging to any Major Hardy was ever berthed at the Le Touquet aerodrome. Your cablegram to-night verified the statement of Hardy as being correct. Now why on earth did you try to deceive me in that respect? You must have known I would have found out soon!"

"I was playing for time," M. Cambon said in a tired voice. "But if you have read the diary, Dacre, you will understand. I assumed that dual personality for a purpose. I was retiring shortly from the *Sûreté*—they knew I was doping myself to death with a foreign drug, and they had already called for my resignation—so I determined to make a big sum of money under an English name. I have bluffed a good many people under that *rôle* of financier—!"

"Yes, but I don't understand," Dacre protested. "Why, in God's name, did you commit those fiendish crimes? I heard two years ago that you had qualified for a pilot's certificate, and that you had turned out an expert flyer, but I kept that knowledge to myself. Now why those ghastly murders? Did your brain go loopy at times?"

The dying man gave a silent nod.

"I went insane under the drug, and when that madness took possession of me—" The voice trailed off into a husky sob.

"One moment," Inspector Murray interrupted. "Better have this glass of water. It might help a little." He had reached for a decanter, and poured out the precious liquid.

The dying man drank it greedily.

It seemed to revive him a trifle.

But the eyes were getting more and more glazed.

"When that madness gripped me," he continued, "I was not responsible for my actions. But no French jury would understand that part of it. You might, Dacre, for I believe you have a bigger heart than most men . . . Those two girls I murdered . . . I met them both here in Weymouth, accosted them in this present disguise, told them I was a rich woman and possessed an airplane, and my plans after that were simple. When the madness came to me, I conceived the horrible design of stabbing them to death in the machine, and then flinging their bodies to earth. But once the murder was committed, I came back to sanity with a rush in each case, and returned to my real self."

"Where did you meet the girls?" Dacre demanded.

"I met the first one near the Pier on Saturday morning last. My machine lay in a convenient field just outside Weymouth, and Ruth Henderson never dreamt that I was other than a woman. I think she fancied I was a trifle eccentric, but that was part of my mile, and I played up to it. It was not the first time I had disguised myself as a woman, and this close-cropped wig of dark hair was really perfect!"

"And Louise Anderson?"

"Ah, I met her before she went to her cousin's house in Portland, and I made her keep our appointment on the Sunday a secret . . . That handbag I picked up one night in a cinema. I was looking for the owner, intending it to serve as an introduction."

Dacre gave a nod of comprehension.

M. Cambon was becoming exhausted.

There was a terrible pain clutching his heart.

"So that was why you set fire to that airplane?" Dacre leaned closer to ask. "You knew there were the marks of blood about the cockpit, and that I, as Yard investigator, would be examining every private plane in the vicinity of Cottingdale!"

"You have said it," Cambon muttered in a low whisper. "But you proved yourself a genius, Dacre, in not giving your big secret away to the last moment. I thought I had hoodwinked you right up to the end. Don't you remember how anxious I was to throw you off the scent in the first case? Ah, what it is to be cursed with a dual personality, my friend. One part of me is M. Cambon, the distinguished expert of the French *Sûreté*; the other is a wild beast drinking human blood like a vampire!"

His eyes closed.

"May God have mercy on your soul," Dacre said quietly.

"Amen to that, sir," Inspector Murray said, as the body of M. Cambon fell limply back.

The end had come!

~ ~ ~ ~ ~

Yes, Lena Somerton secured her stupendous scoop for the *Sentinel*, but that was really not the biggest prize she won.

Three weeks later, she slipped into the back seat of the Avro airplane at Cottingdale, not merely as a famous lady journalist but as the newly wed wife of Malcolm Dacre, the distinguished Scotland Yard expert, and the individual who took control of the joy-stick was no other than Dacre himself, as he clambered into the front seat.

It was destined to be a glorious honeymoon!

THE END

RAMBLE HOUSE's

HARRY STEPHEN KEELER WEBWORK MYSTERIES

(RH) indicates the title is available ONLY in the RAMBLE HOUSE edition

The Ace of Spades Murder
The Affair of the Bottled Deuce (RH)
The Amazing Web
The Barking Clock
Behind That Mask
The Book with the Orange Leaves
The Bottle with the Green Wax Seal
The Box from Japan
The Case of the Canny Killer
The Case of the Crazy Corpse (RH)
The Case of the Flying Hands (RH)
The Case of the Ivory Arrow
The Case of the Jeweled Ragpicker
The Case of the Lavender Gripsack
The Case of the Mysterious Moll
The Case of the 16 Beans
The Case of the Transparent Nude (RH)
The Case of the Transposed Legs
The Case of the Two-Headed Idiot (RH)
The Case of the Two Strange Ladies
The Circus Stealers (RH)
Cleopatra's Tears
A Copy of Beowulf (RH)
The Crimson Cube (RH)
The Face of the Man From Saturn
Find the Clock
The Five Silver Buddhas
The 4th King
The Gallows Waits, My Lord! (RH)
The Green Jade Hand
Finger! Finger!
Hangman's Nights (RH)
I, Chameleon (RH)
I Killed Lincoln at 10:13! (RH)
The Iron Ring
The Man Who Changed His Skin (RH)
The Man with the Crimson Box
The Man with the Magic Eardrums
The Man with the Wooden Spectacles
The Marceau Case
The Matilda Hunter Murder
The Monocled Monster
The Murder of London Lew
The Murdered Mathematician
The Mysterious Card (RH)
The Mysterious Ivory Ball of Wong Shing Li (RH)
The Mystery of the Fiddling Cracksman
The Peacock Fan
The Photo of Lady X (RH)
The Portrait of Jirjohn Cobb
Report on Vanessa Hewstone (RH)
Riddle of the Travelling Skull
Riddle of the Wooden Parrakeet (RH)
The Scarlet Mummy (RH)
The Search for X-Y-Z
The Sharkskin Book
Sing Sing Nights
The Six From Nowhere (RH)
The Skull of the Waltzing Clown
The Spectacles of Mr. Cagliostro
Stand By—London Calling!
The Steeltown Strangler
The Stolen Gravestone (RH)
Strange Journey (RH)
The Strange Will
The Straw Hat Murders (RH)
The Street of 1000 Eyes (RH)
Thieves' Nights
Three Novellos (RH)
The Tiger Snake
The Trap (RH)
Vagabond Nights (Defrauded Yeggman)
Vagabond Nights 2 (10 Hours)
The Vanishing Gold Truck
The Voice of the Seven Sparrows
The Washington Square Enigma
When Thief Meets Thief
The White Circle (RH)
The Wonderful Scheme of Mr. Christopher Thorne
X. Jones—of Scotland Yard
Y. Cheung, Business Detective

Keeler Related Works

A To Izzard: A Harry Stephen Keeler Companion by Fender Tucker — Articles and stories about Harry, by Harry, and in his style. Included is a compleat bibliography.

Wild About Harry: Reviews of Keeler Novels — Edited by Richard Polt & Fender Tucker — 22 reviews of works by Harry Stephen Keeler from *Keeler News*. A perfect introduction to the author.

The Keeler Keyhole Collection: Annotated newsletter rants from Harry Stephen Keeler, edited by Francis M. Nevins. Over 400 pages of incredibly personal Keeleriana.

Fakealoo — Pastiches of the style of Harry Stephen Keeler by selected demented members of the HSK Society. Updated every year with the new winner.

Strands of the Web: Short Stories of Harry Stephen Keeler — 29 stories, just about all that Keeler wrote, are edited and introduced by Fred Cleaver.

RAMBLE HOUSE's LOON SANCTUARY

A Clear Path to Cross — Sharon Knowles short mystery stories by Ed Lynskey.
A Corpse Walks in Brooklyn and Other Stories — Volume 5 in the Day Keene in the Detective Pulps series.
A Jimmy Starr Omnibus — Three 40s novels by Jimmy Starr.
A Niche in Time and Other Stories — Classic SF by William F. Temple
A Roland Daniel Double: The Signal and The Return of Wu Fang — Classic thrillers from the 30s.
A Shot Rang Out — Three decades of reviews and articles by today's Anthony Boucher, Jon Breen. An essential book for any mystery lover's library.
A Smell of Smoke — A 1951 English countryside thriller by Miles Burton.
A Snark Selection — Lewis Carroll's *The Hunting of the Snark* with two Snarkian chapters by Harry Stephen Keeler — Illustrated by Gavin L. O'Keefe.
A Young Man's Heart — A forgotten early classic by Cornell Woolrich.
Alexander Laing Novels — *The Motives of Nicholas Holtz* and *Dr. Scarlett*, stories of medical mayhem and intrigue from the 30s.
An Angel in the Street — Modern hardboiled noir by Peter Genovese.
Automaton — Brilliant treatise on robotics: 1928-style! By H. Stafford Hatfield.
Away From the Here and Now — Clare Winger Harris stories, collected by Richard A. Lupoff
Beast or Man? — A 1930 novel of racism and horror by Sean M'Guire. Introduced by John Pelan.
Black Beadle — A 1939 thriller by E.C.R. Lorac.
Black Hogan Strikes Again — Australia's Peter Renwick pens a tale of the 30s outback.
Black River Falls — Suspense from the master, Ed Gorman.
Blondy's Boy Friend — A snappy 1930 story by Philip Wylie, writing as Leatrice Homesley.
Blood in a Snap — The *Finnegan's Wake* of the 21st century, by Jim Weiler.
Blood Moon — The first of the Robert Payne series by Ed Gorman.
Bogart '48 — Hollywood action with Bogie by John Stanley and Kenn Davis
Calling Lou Largo! — Two Lou Largo novels by William Ard.
Cornucopia of Crime — Francis M. Nevins assembled this huge collection of his writings about crime literature and the people who write it. Essential for any serious mystery library.
Corpse Without Flesh — Strange novel of forensics by George Bruce
Crimson Clown Novels — By Johnston McCulley, author of the Zorro novels, *The Crimson Clown* and *The Crimson Clown Again.*
Dago Red — 22 tales of dark suspense by Bill Pronzini.
Dark Sanctuary — Weird Menace story by H. B. Gregory
David Hume Novels — *Corpses Never Argue, Cemetery First Stop, Make Way for the Mourners, Eternity Here I Come*. 1930s British hardboiled fiction with an attitude.
Dead Man Talks Too Much — Hollywood boozer by Weed Dickenson.
Death Leaves No Card — One of the most unusual murdered-in-the-tub mysteries you'll ever read. By Miles Burton.
Death March of the Dancing Dolls and Other Stories — Volume Three in the Day Keene in the Detective Pulps series. Introduced by Bill Crider.
Deep Space and other Stories — A collection of SF gems by Richard A. Lupoff.
Detective Duff Unravels It — Episodic mysteries by Harvey O'Higgins.
Diabolic Candelabra — Classic 30s mystery by E.R. Punshon
Dictator's Way — Another D.S. Bobby Owen mystery from E.R. Punshon
Dime Novels: Ramble House's 10-Cent Books — *Knife in the Dark* by Robert Leslie Bellem, *Hot Lead* and *Song of Death* by Ed Earl Repp, *A Hashish House in New York* by H.H. Kane, and five more.
Doctor Arnoldi — Tiffany Thayer's story of the death of death.
Don Diablo: Book of a Lost Film — Two-volume treatment of a western by Paul Landres, with diagrams. Intro by Francis M. Nevins.
Dope and Swastikas — Two strange novels from 1922 by Edmund Snell
Dope Tales #1 — Two dope-riddled classics; *Dope Runners* by Gerald Grantham and *Death Takes the Joystick* by Phillip Condé.

Dope Tales #2 — Two more narco-classics; *The Invisible Hand* by Rex Dark and *The Smokers of Hashish* by Norman Berrow.
Dope Tales #3 — Two enchanting novels of opium by the master, Sax Rohmer. *Dope* and *The Yellow Claw.*
Double Hot — Two 60s softcore sex novels by Morris Hershman.
Double Sex — Yet two more panting thrillers from Morris Hershman.
Dr. Odin — Douglas Newton's 1933 racial potboiler comes back to life.
Evangelical Cockroach — Jack Woodford writes about writing.
Evidence in Blue — 1938 mystery by E. Charles Vivian.
Fatal Accident — Murder by automobile, a 1936 mystery by Cecil M. Wills.
Fighting Mad — Todd Robbins' 1922 novel about boxing and life
Finger-prints Never Lie — A 1939 classic detective novel by John G. Brandon.
Freaks and Fantasies — Eerie tales by Tod Robbins, collaborator of Tod Browning on the film FREAKS.
Gadsby — A lipogram (a novel without the letter E). Ernest Vincent Wright's last work, published in 1939 right before his death.
Gelett Burgess Novels — *The Master of Mysteries, The White Cat, Two O'Clock Courage, Ladies in Boxes, Find the Woman, The Heart Line, The Picaroons* and *Lady Mechante.* Recently added is A Gelett Burgess Sampler, edited by Alfred Jan. All are introduced by Richard A. Lupoff.
Geronimo — S. M. Barrett's 1905 autobiography of a noble American.
Hake Talbot Novels — *Rim of the Pit, The Hangman's Handyman.* Classic locked room mysteries, with mapback covers by Gavin O'Keefe.
Hands Out of Hell and Other Stories — John H. Knox's eerie hallucinations
Hell is a City — William Ard's masterpiece.
Hollywood Dreams — A novel of Tinsel Town and the Depression by Richard O'Brien.
Hostesses in Hell and Other Stories — Russell Gray's most graphic stories
House of the Restless Dead — Strange and ominous tales by Hugh B. Cave
I Stole $16,000,000 — A true story by cracksman Herbert E. Wilson.
Inclination to Murder — 1966 thriller by New Zealand's Harriet Hunter.
Invaders from the Dark — Classic werewolf tale from Greye La Spina.
J. Poindexter, Colored — Classic satirical black novel by Irvin S. Cobb.
Jack Mann Novels — Strange murder in the English countryside. *Gees' First Case, Nightmare Farm, Grey Shapes, The Ninth Life, The Glass Too Many, Her Ways Are Death, The Kleinert Case* and *Maker of Shadows.*
Jake Hardy — A lusty western tale from Wesley Tallant.
Jim Harmon Double Novels — *Vixen Hollow/Celluloid Scandal, The Man Who Made Maniacs/Silent Siren, Ape Rape/Wanton Witch, Sex Burns Like Fire/Twist Session, Sudden Lust/Passion Strip, Sin Unlimited/Harlot Master, Twilight Girls/Sex Institution.* Written in the early 60s and never reprinted until now.
Joel Townsley Rogers Novels and Short Stories — By the author of *The Red Right Hand: Once In a Red Moon, Lady With the Dice, The Stopped Clock, Never Leave My Bed.* Also two short story collections: *Night of Horror* and *Killing Time.*
John Carstairs, Space Detective — Arboreal Sci-fi by Frank Belknap Long
Joseph Shallit Novels — *The Case of the Billion Dollar Body, Lady Don't Die on My Doorstep, Kiss the Killer, Yell Bloody Murder, Take Your Last Look.* One of America's best 50's authors and a favorite of author Bill Pronzini.
Keller Memento — 45 short stories of the amazing and weird by Dr. David Keller.
Killer's Caress — Cary Moran's 1936 hardboiled thriller.
Lady of the Yellow Death and Other Stories — More stories by Wyatt Blassingame.
League of the Grateful Dead and Other Stories — Volume One in the Day Keene in the Detective Pulps series.
Library of Death — Ghastly tale by Ronald S. L. Harding, introduced by John Pelan
Malcolm Jameson Novels and Short Stories — *Astonishing! Astounding!, Tarnished Bomb, The Alien Envoy and Other Stories* and *The Chariots of San Fernando and Other Stories.* All introduced and edited by John Pelan or Richard A. Lupoff.
Man Out of Hell and Other Stories — Volume II of the John H. Knox weird pulps collection.
Marblehead: A Novel of H.P. Lovecraft — A long-lost masterpiece from Richard A. Lupoff. This is the "director's cut", the long version that has never been published before.

Mark of the Laughing Death and Other Stories — Shockers from the pulps by Francis James, introduced by John Pelan.

Master of Souls — Mark Hansom's 1937 shocker is introduced by weirdologist John Pelan.

Max Afford Novels — *Owl of Darkness, Death's Mannikins, Blood on His Hands, The Dead Are Blind, The Sheep and the Wolves, Sinners in Paradise* and *Two Locked Room Mysteries and a Ripping Yarn* by one of Australia's finest mystery novelists.

Money Brawl — Two books about the writing business by Jack Woodford and H. Bedford-Jones. Introduced by Richard A. Lupoff.

More Secret Adventures of Sherlock Holmes — Gary Lovisi's second collection of tales about the unknown sides of the great detective.

Muddled Mind: Complete Works of Ed Wood, Jr. — David Hayes and Hayden Davis deconstruct the life and works of the mad, but canny, genius.

Murder among the Nudists — A mystery from 1934 by Peter Hunt, featuring a naked Detective-Inspector going undercover in a nudist colony.

Murder in Black and White — 1931 classic tennis whodunit by Evelyn Elder.

Murder in Shawnee — Two novels of the Alleghenies by John Douglas: *Shawnee Alley Fire* and *Haunts.*

Murder in Silk — A 1937 Yellow Peril novel of the silk trade by Ralph Trevor.

My Deadly Angel — 1955 Cold War drama by John Chelton.

My First Time: The One Experience You Never Forget — Michael Birchwood — 64 true first-person narratives of how they lost it.

Mysterious Martin, the Master of Murder — Two versions of a strange 1912 novel by Tod Robbins about a man who writes books that can kill.

Norman Berrow Novels — *The Bishop's Sword, Ghost House, Don't Go Out After Dark, Claws of the Cougar, The Smokers of Hashish, The Secret Dancer, Don't Jump Mr. Boland!, The Footprints of Satan, Fingers for Ransom, The Three Tiers of Fantasy, The Spaniard's Thumb, The Eleventh Plague, Words Have Wings, One Thrilling Night, The Lady's in Danger, It Howls at Night, The Terror in the Fog, Oil Under the Window, Murder in the Melody, The Singing Room.* This is the complete Norman Berrow library of locked-room mysteries, several of which are masterpieces.

Old Faithful and Other Stories — SF classic tales by Raymond Z. Gallun

Old Times' Sake — Short stories by James Reasoner from Mike Shayne Magazine.

One Dreadful Night — A classic mystery by Ronald S. L. Harding

Pair O' Jacks — A mystery novel and a diatribe about publishing by Jack Woodford

Perfect .38 — Two early Timothy Dane novels by William Ard. More to come.

Prince Pax — Devilish intrigue by George Sylvester Viereck and Philip Eldridge

Prose Bowl — Futuristic satire of a world where hack writing has replaced football as our national obsession, by Bill Pronzini and Barry N. Malzberg.

Red Light — The history of legal prostitution in Shreveport Louisiana by Eric Brock. Includes wonderful photos of the houses and the ladies.

Researching American-Made Toy Soldiers — A 276-page collection of a lifetime of articles by toy soldier expert Richard O'Brien.

Reunion in Hell — Volume One of the John H. Knox series of weird stories from the pulps. Introduced by horror expert John Pelan.

Ripped from the Headlines! — The Jack the Ripper story as told in the newspaper articles in the *New York* and *London Times.*

Rough Cut & New, Improved Murder — Ed Gorman's first two novels.

R.R. Ryan Novels — Freak Museum and The Subjugated Beast, two horror classics.

Ruby of a Thousand Dreams — The villain Wu Fang returns in this Roland Daniel novel.

Ruled By Radio — 1925 futuristic novel by Robert L. Hadfield & Frank E. Farncombe.

Rupert Penny Novels — *Policeman's Holiday, Policeman's Evidence, Lucky Policeman, Policeman in Armour, Sealed Room Murder, Sweet Poison, The Talkative Policeman, She had to Have Gas* and *Cut and Run* (by Martin Tanner.) Rupert Penny is the pseudonym of Australian Charles Thornett, a master of the locked room, impossible crime plot.

Sacred Locomotive Flies — Richard A. Lupoff's psychedelic SF story.

Sam — Early gay novel by Lonnie Coleman.

Sand's Game — Spectacular hard-boiled noir from Ennis Willie, edited by Lynn Myers and Stephen Mertz, with contributions from Max Allan Collins, Bill Crider, Wayne Dundee, Bill Pronzini, Gary Lovisi and James Reasoner.
Sand's War — More violent fiction from the typewriter of Ennis Willie
Satan's Den Exposed — True crime in Truth or Consequences New Mexico — Award-winning journalism by the *Desert Journal.*
Satans of Saturn — Novellas from the pulps by Otis Adelbert Kline and E. H. Price
Satan's Sin House and Other Stories — Horrific gore by Wayne Rogers
Secrets of a Teenage Superhero — Graphic lit by Jonathan Sweet
Sex Slave — Potboiler of lust in the days of Cleopatra by Dion Leclerq, 1966.
Sideslip — 1968 SF masterpiece by Ted White and Dave Van Arnam.
Slammer Days — Two full-length prison memoirs: *Men into Beasts* (1952) by George Sylvester Viereck and *Home Away From Home* (1962) by Jack Woodford.
Slippery Staircase — 1930s whodunit from E.C.R. Lorac
Sorcerer's Chessmen — John Pelan introduces this 1939 classic by Mark Hansom.
Star Griffin — Michael Kurland's 1987 masterpiece of SF drollery is back.
Stakeout on Millennium Drive — Award-winning Indianapolis Noir by Ian Woollen.
Strands of the Web: Short Stories of Harry Stephen Keeler — Edited and Introduced by Fred Cleaver.
Summer Camp for Corpses and Other Stories — Weird Menace tales from Arthur Leo Zagat; introduced by John Pelan.
Suzy — A collection of comic strips by Richard O'Brien and Bob Vojtko from 1970.
Tales of the Macabre and Ordinary — Modern twisted horror by Chris Mikul, author of the *Bizarrism* series.
Tales of Terror and Torment #1 — John Pelan selects and introduces this sampler of weird menace tales from the pulps.
Tenebrae — Ernest G. Henham's 1898 horror tale brought back.
The Amorous Intrigues & Adventures of Aaron Burr — by Anonymous. Hot historical action about the man who almost became Emperor of Mexico.
The Anthony Boucher Chronicles — edited by Francis M. Nevins. Book reviews by Anthony Boucher written for the *San Francisco Chronicle,* 1942 – 1947. Essential and fascinating reading by the best book reviewer there ever was.
The Barclay Catalogs — Two essential books about toy soldier collecting by Richard O'Brien
The Basil Wells Omnibus — A collection of Wells' stories by Richard A. Lupoff
The Beautiful Dead and Other Stories — Dreadful tales from Donald Dale
The Best of 10-Story Book — edited by Chris Mikul, over 35 stories from the literary magazine Harry Stephen Keeler edited.
The Black Dark Murders — Vintage 50s college murder yarn by Milt Ozaki, writing as Robert O. Saber.
The Book of Time — The classic novel by H.G. Wells is joined by sequels by Wells himself and three stories by Richard A. Lupoff. Illustrated by Gavin L. O'Keefe.
The Case in the Clinic — One of E.C.R. Lorac's finest.
The Strange Case of the Antlered Man — A mystery of superstition by Edwy Searles Brooks.
The Case of the Bearded Bride — #4 in the Day Keene in the Detective Pulps series
The Case of the Little Green Men — Mack Reynolds wrote this love song to sci-fi fans back in 1951 and it's now back in print.
The Case of the Withered Hand — 1936 potboiler by John G. Brandon.
The Charlie Chaplin Murder Mystery — A 2004 tribute by noted film scholar, Wes D. Gehring.
The Chinese Jar Mystery — Murder in the manor by John Stephen Strange, 1934.
The Cloudbuilders and Other Stories — SF tales from Colin Kapp.
The Compleat Calhoon — All of Fender Tucker's works: Includes *Totah Six-Pack, Weed, Women and Song* and *Tales from the Tower,* plus a CD of all of his songs.
The Compleat Ova Hamlet — Parodies of SF authors by Richard A. Lupoff. This is a brand new edition with more stories and more illustrations by Trina Robbins.
The Contested Earth and Other SF Stories — A never-before published space opera and seven short stories by Jim Harmon.
The Crimson Query — A 1929 thriller from Arlton Eadie. A perfect way to get introduced.

The Curse of Cantire — Classic 1939 novel of a family curse by Walter S. Masterman.
The Devil and the C.I.D. — Odd diabolic mystery by E.C.R. Lorac
The Devil Drives — An odd prison and lost treasure novel from 1932 by Virgil Markham.
The Devil of Pei-Ling — Herbert Asbury's 1929 tale of the occult.
The Devil's Mistress — A 1915 Scottish gothic tale by J. W. Brodie-Innes, a member of Aleister Crowley's Golden Dawn.
The Devil's Nightclub and Other Stories — John Pelan introduces some gruesome tales by Nat Schachner.
The Disentanglers — Episodic intrigue at the turn of last century by Andrew Lang
The Dog Poker Code — A spoof of *The Da Vinci Code* by D.B. Smithee.
The Dumpling — Political murder from 1907 by Coulson Kernahan.
The End of It All and Other Stories — Ed Gorman selected his favorite short stories for this huge collection.
The Fangs of Suet Pudding — A 1944 novel of the German invasion by Adams Farr
The Finger of Destiny and Other Stories — Edmund Snell's superb collection of weird stories of Borneo.
The Ghost of Gaston Revere — From 1935, a novel of life and beyond by Mark Hansom, introduced by John Pelan.
The Girl in the Dark — A thriller from Roland Daniel
The Gold Star Line — Seaboard adventure from L.T. Reade and Robert Eustace.
The Golden Dagger — 1951 Scotland Yard yarn by E. R. Punshon.
The Great Orme Terror — Horror stories by Garnett Radcliffe from the pulps
The Hairbreadth Escapes of Major Mendax — Francis Blake Crofton's 1889 boys' book.
The House That Time Forgot and Other Stories — Insane pulpitude by Robert F. Young
The House of the Vampire — 1907 poetic thriller by George S. Viereck.
The Illustrious Corpse — Murder hijinx from Tiffany Thayer
The Incredible Adventures of Rowland Hern — Intriguing 1928 impossible crimes by Nicholas Olde.
The Julius Caesar Murder Case — A classic 1935 re-telling of the assassination by Wallace Irwin that's much more fun than the Shakespeare version.
The Koky Comics — A collection of all of the 1978-1981 Sunday and daily comic strips by Richard O'Brien and Mort Gerberg, in two volumes.
The Lady of the Terraces — 1925 missing race adventure by E. Charles Vivian.
The Lord of Terror — 1925 mystery with master-criminal, Fantômas.
The Melamare Mystery — A classic 1929 Arsene Lupin mystery by Maurice Leblanc
The Man Who Was Secrett — Epic SF stories from John Brunner
The Man Without a Planet — Science fiction tales by Richard Wilson
The N. R. De Mexico Novels — Robert Bragg, the real N.R. de Mexico, presents *Marijuana Girl, Madman on a Drum, Private Chauffeur* in one volume.
The Night Remembers — A 1991 Jack Walsh mystery from Ed Gorman.
The One After Snelling — Kickass modern noir from Richard O'Brien.
The Organ Reader — A huge compilation of just about everything published in the 1971-1972 radical bay-area newspaper, *THE ORGAN*. A coffee table book that points out the shallowness of the coffee table mindset.
The Poker Club — Three in one! Ed Gorman's ground-breaking novel, the short story it was based upon, and the screenplay of the film made from it.
The Private Journal & Diary of John H. Surratt — The memoirs of the man who conspired to assassinate President Lincoln.
The Ramble House Mapbacks — Recently revised book by Gavin L. O'Keefe with color pictures of all the Ramble House books with mapbacks.
The Secret Adventures of Sherlock Holmes — Three Sherlockian pastiches by the Brooklyn author/publisher, Gary Lovisi.
The Shadow on the House — Mark Hansom's 1934 masterpiece of horror is introduced by John Pelan.
The Sign of the Scorpion — A 1935 Edmund Snell tale of oriental evil.
The Singular Problem of the Stygian House-Boat — Two classic tales by John Kendrick Bangs about the denizens of Hades.
The Smiling Corpse — Philip Wylie and Bernard Bergman's odd 1935 novel.

The Spider: Satan's Murder Machines — A thesis about Iron Man
The Stench of Death: An Odoriferous Omnibus by Jack Moskovitz — Two complete novels and two novellas from 60's sleaze author, Jack Moskovitz.
The Story Writer and Other Stories — Classic SF from Richard Wilson
The Strange Case of the Antlered Man — 1935 dementia from Edwy Searles Brooks
The Strange Thirteen — Richard B. Gamon's odd stories about Raj India.
The Technique of the Mystery Story — Carolyn Wells' tips about writing.
The Threat of Nostalgia — A collection of his most obscure stories by Jon Breen
The Time Armada — Fox B. Holden's 1953 SF gem.
The Tongueless Horror and Other Stories — Volume One of the series of short stories from the weird pulps by Wyatt Blassingame.
The Town from Planet Five — From Richard Wilson, two SF classics, *And Then the Town Took Off* and *The Girls from Planet 5*
The Tracer of Lost Persons — From 1906, an episodic novel that became a hit radio series in the 30s. Introduced by Richard A. Lupoff.
The Trail of the Cloven Hoof — Diabolical horror from 1935 by Arlton Eadie. Introduced by John Pelan.
The Triune Man — Mindscrambling science fiction from Richard A. Lupoff.
The Unholy Goddess and Other Stories — Wyatt Blassingame's first DTP compilation
The Universal Holmes — Richard A. Lupoff's 2007 collection of five Holmesian pastiches and a recipe for giant rat stew.
The Werewolf vs the Vampire Woman — Hard to believe ultraviolence by either Arthur M. Scarm or Arthur M. Scram.
The Whistling Ancestors — A 1936 classic of weirdness by Richard E. Goddard and introduced by John Pelan.
The White Owl — A vintage thriller from Edmund Snell
The White Peril in the Far East — Sidney Lewis Gulick's 1905 indictment of the West and assurance that Japan would never attack the U.S.
The Wizard of Berner's Abbey — A 1935 horror gem written by Mark Hansom and introduced by John Pelan.
The Wonderful Wizard of Oz — by L. Frank Baum and illustrated by Gavin L. O'Keefe
Through the Looking Glass — Lewis Carroll wrote it; Gavin L. O'Keefe illustrated it.
Time Line — Ramble House artist Gavin O'Keefe selects his most evocative art inspired by the twisted literature he reads and designs.
Tiresias — Psychotic modern horror novel by Jonathan M. Sweet.
Tortures and Towers — Two novellas of terror by Dexter Dayle.
Totah Six-Pack — Fender Tucker's six tales about Farmington in one sleek volume.
Tree of Life, Book of Death — Grania Davis' book of her life.
Triple Quest — An arty mystery from the 30s by E.R. Punshon.
Trail of the Spirit Warrior — Roger Haley's saga of life in the Indian Territories.
Two Kinds of Bad — Two 50s novels by William Ard about Danny Fontaine
Two Suns of Morcali and Other Stories — Evelyn E. Smith's SF tour-de-force
Ultra-Boiled — 23 gut-wrenching tales by our Man in Brooklyn, Gary Lovisi.
Up Front From Behind — A 2011 satire of Wall Street by James B. Kobak.
Victims & Villains — Intriguing Sherlockiana from Derham Groves.
Wade Wright Novels — *Echo of Fear, Death At Nostalgia Street, It Leads to Murder* and *Shadows' Edge*, a double book featuring *Shadows Don't Bleed* and *The Sharp Edge*.
Walter S. Masterman Novels — *The Green Toad, The Flying Beast, The Yellow Mistletoe, The Wrong Verdict, The Perjured Alibi, The Border Line, The Bloodhounds Bay, The Curse of Cantire* and *The Baddington Horror.* Masterman wrote horror and mystery, some introduced by John Pelan.
We Are the Dead and Other Stories — Volume Two in the Day Keene in the Detective Pulps series, introduced by Ed Gorman. When done, there may be 11 in the series.
Welsh Rarebit Tales — Charming stories from 1902 by Harle Oren Cummins
West Texas War and Other Western Stories — by Gary Lovisi.
What If? Volume 1, 2 and 3 — Richard A. Lupoff introduces three decades worth of SF short stories that should have won a Hugo, but didn't.
When the Batman Thirsts and Other Stories — Weird tales from Frederick C. Davis.
Whip Dodge: Man Hunter — Wesley Tallant's saga of a bounty hunter of the old West.

Win, Place and Die! — The first new mystery by Milt Ozaki in decades. The ultimate novel of 70s Reno.

Writer 1 and 2 — A magnus opus from Richard A. Lupoff summing up his life as writer.

You'll Die Laughing — Bruce Elliott's 1945 novel of murder at a practical joker's English countryside manor.

RAMBLE HOUSE

Fender Tucker, Prop. Gavin L. O'Keefe, Graphics

www.ramblehouse.com fender@ramblehouse.com

228-826-1783 10329 Sheephead Drive, Vancleave MS 39565

Printed in Great Britain
by Amazon

33882206R00116